Brenda Jackson is a *New York Times* bestselling author of more than one hundred romance titles. Brenda lives in Jacksonville, Florida, and divides her time between family, writing and travelling.

Email Brenda at authorbrendajackson@gmail.com or visit her on her website at brendajackson.net.

His to Claim

BRENDA JACKSON

MILLS & BOON

First published in Great Britain 2019
by Mills & Boon, an imprint of HarperCollins*Publishers*
1 London Bridge Street, London, SE1 9GF

Large Print edition 2019

© 2019 Brenda Streater Jackson

ISBN: 978-0-263-08366-8

MIX
Paper from
responsible sources
FSC® C007454

This book is produced from independently certified
FSC™ paper to ensure responsible forest management. For
more information visit www.harpercollins.co.uk/green.

Printed and bound in Great Britain
by CPI Group (UK) Ltd, Croydon, CR0 4YY

Acknowledgements

To the man who will always
and forever be the love of my life
and the wind beneath my wings:
Gerald Jackson, Sr.

Special thanks to my readers who are
attending the Brenda Jackson Readers
Reunion 2019 as we cruise to Aruba.
Fun! Fun! Fun! I always enjoy
spending time with you!

To all my readers who requested
Mac's story. This book is for you.

Sending congratulations to my
goddaughter, Ty'ra Malloy, who
is celebrating her graduation from
Florida State University. Your Goddy
is very proud of you!

Though thy beginning was small, yet
thy latter end should greatly increase.
—*Job* 8:7

One

Thurston McRoy, called Mac by all who knew him, got out of his rental vehicle and slid the keys into the pocket of his jeans. There was a dark blue sedan parked in his driveway.

At two in the morning.

It looked like a brand-new luxury Lexus and had a Georgia license plate. The only people he knew who lived in Georgia were his parents. Was this their vehicle?

They would often visit Virginia to check on his wife, Teri, and the kids whenever he was away for long periods of time. With his work as a navy SEAL, he often took part in missions where he was out of communication with his family. He appreciated his parents for all they did to make his work easier on his family. However, he was surprised to see their car here, tonight. Over the last year or so, they'd begun staying at a nearby hotel whenever they came to town. Unfortunately, there were no longer any spare rooms at the McRoy house.

The last time Mac had come home, he'd discovered Teri had given Tia, their oldest daughter of nine, her own room—namely the spare room. According to Teri, Tia was at the age where she now wanted privacy from her three younger sisters, Tatum, Tempest and Tasha. But did she have to take the only spare room in the house? The one that doubled as his man cave whenever he came home?

He and Teri had always talked about buying a bigger place. Frankly, he had more than enough means to make it happen thanks to the investments he'd made on the advice of his friend and teammate, Bane Westmoreland. However, over the past several years, he'd been gone a lot, sent on several missions, and he was too hands-on to even think of letting her make such a major purchase like that without him. He knew exactly what he wanted in a home and Teri knew what she wanted. And their wants were on the opposite ends of the spectrum. She wanted a two-story home and he wanted ranch style. The fewer stairs he had to climb, the better.

Tonight, he was returning home from an eight-month-long, highly classified covert operation near Libya. During that time, he hadn't been able to let anyone, not even Teri, know of his whereabouts. He had left home in the wee hours of the morning after making passionate love to his wife, without being able to tell her where he was going or when he would return.

As a toddler he recalled sitting on his maternal grandfather's knee and listening to stories of his military days, specifically as a SEAL. His paternal grandfather had been a military man, as well, an army ranger. Although Mac's father hadn't been in the military Mac had decided early in life protecting his country was something he wanted to do. Being a SEAL had always been his dream and he'd worked hard to make that particular dream come true. Now after almost twenty years whenever he thought it was time to retire, a part of him was convinced there was one more mission, one more opportunity to defend the country he loved.

The last operation had been brutal, but all the members of his team were alive and accounted for. Now he was glad to be back home with his wife and kids, and as much as he loved his parents, he hadn't counted on having any company. He needed a cold beer and his wife. Not necessarily in that order.

He figured everyone was in bed, yet an uneasy feeling crept over him as he entered his home. He paused in the foyer. Was that the television he heard coming from the living room? Typically, Teri would be in bed before ten because she got up around six to jumpstart her day.

Tatum was seven and attended a different school than Tia. Tempest was five and attended kindergarten at the same school as Tatum. Tasha, their baby, who was barely three, attended day care. He hadn't liked the idea of Tasha in day care, but Teri claimed Tasha needed to be around kids her age at least a few days a week to start developing her social skills.

Mac hadn't wanted Teri to work outside the home, either, but she'd insisted that she needed to get out of the house for a while during the day. So now she was working part-time at one of the libraries in town.

Mindful of not waking the kids, while at the same time intent on not scaring his parents, he took out his phone and texted Teri. She practically slept with the phone beside her. When the message didn't immediately show as delivered, he frowned, wondering what was wrong with her phone. He'd tried calling her earlier, twice in fact, when his plane had landed in DC. He hadn't gotten an answer either time.

What was going on?

He placed his gear down and was headed toward his bedroom when his father rounded the corner. Carlton McRoy nearly jumped out of his skin when he saw his son.

"Damn it, Mac, you trying to give me heart failure?" his father asked. "I didn't hear you come in."

Mac crossed the floor to give his father a

bear hug. "You weren't supposed to hear me. I'm a SEAL, Dad."

"Why didn't you ring the doorbell?"

Mac thought that was a crazy question. "I live here. I don't need to ring the doorbell. Besides, I didn't want to wake anyone. By the way, I like your new set of wheels."

His father beamed. "Thanks. It's your mom's car. I surprised her with it as an early anniversary gift. It's been almost forty years, you know."

Yes, Mac knew. He was the oldest of two and Carlton and Alexis Youngblood-McRoy hadn't wasted any time after their wedding to start a family. He'd been born a week shy of their first anniversary. He figured he was supposed to be one and done, but his sister Kylie had been born on his parents' tenth anniversary. "That's a nice gift."

"I thought so, and Lex was more than deserving," his father said.

Mac smiled. His parents were special. There weren't two adults he admired more and they had always been great role models for him and his sister. Their interracial marriage had worked for them because they'd always said love got them together and it would be love that kept them together.

"Thurston!"

Mac glanced around and chuckled when his mother practically threw herself into his arms. "Hey, Mom," he said, placing a kiss on her cheek.

"I heard voices and thought one of the girls had awakened."

"No, it's just me and Dad. He saw me when I was headed down the hall to my bedroom to let Teri know I was home."

He still had his arms around his mother's shoulders when he felt her tense up. "Mom? You okay?" he asked, looking down at her.

He thought the same thing now that he'd thought while growing up. His mother was a beautiful woman with eyes a unique shade of blue and ash-blond hair. His father had a dark chocolate complexion, which accounted for Mac and his younger sister's skin tone being a combination of the two.

When his mother still hadn't answered his question, he turned his eyes to his father, who had the same wary expression on his face that Mac's mother wore. Releasing his arm from around his mother's shoulder, Mac straightened to his full height of six feet three inches. "Okay, what's going on?"

When his parents glanced at each other, that uneasy feeling from earlier crept over him again. Not liking it, he turned to go down the hall toward his bedroom when his father reached out to stop him.

"Teri isn't here, Mac."

Mac turned back to his father. His mother had moved to stand beside his dad. "It's after two in the morning and tomorrow is a school day for the girls. So where is she?"

His mother reached out and touched his arm. "She needed to get away and she asked if we would come keep the girls."

Mac frowned. He knew his wife. She would not have gone anywhere without their daughters. "What do you mean she needed to get away? Why?"

"She's the one who has to tell you that, Thurston. It's not for us to say."

His mother looked up at him with an uncomfortable expression on her face. His gaze left his mother and moved over to his father, who was wearing the same look.

"What's going on, Dad? Mom? Why can't you tell me the reason Teri felt she had to get away?"

"Because it's not our place to do so, son."

Mac drew in a deep breath, not understanding any of this. Because his parents were acting so secretive, he felt his confusion and anger escalating. "Fine. Where is she?"

It was his father who spoke. "She left three days ago for the Torchlight Dude Ranch."

Mac's frown deepened. "The Torchlight Dude Ranch? In Wyoming?"

"Yes."

"What the hell did she go there for?"

His father didn't say anything for a minute and then gave Mac an answer. "She said she always wanted to go back there."

Mac rubbed his hand across his face. Yes, Teri had always wanted to go back there, the place he'd taken her on their honeymoon a little over ten years ago. And he'd always promised to take her back. But between his covert missions and their growing family, there had never been enough time. Teri, who'd been raised on a ranch in Texas, was a cowgirl at heart and for a short while had competed on the rodeo circuit due to her roping and riding skills. She'd even represented the state of Texas as a rodeo queen before they'd met.

When they'd married, she had given it all up to travel around the world with her naval husband. She'd said she'd done so gladly. Why in the world would Teri leave their kids and go to a dude ranch by herself?

He knew the only person who could answer that question was Teri.

"I tried calling her twice from the airport and she's not answering her phone," he finally said, his tone truly filled with anger now.

"She probably couldn't. We talk to her every day when she calls to check on the girls. The reception at the dude ranch is not good and she has to drive into town to call out. Teri usually phones us around five every evening. I'm sure she'll be calling today as usual, so you'll get a chance to talk to her," his mother said, smiling.

He stared at his parents. Did they honestly think he intended to hang around and wait for Teri's call?

"I want to see the girls. I won't wake them, but I need to see them before I leave."

"Leave?" his father asked, looking at him strangely.

"Yes, leave."

"Where are you going?" his mother asked.

He met their gazes. "I'm going to the Torch-light Dude Ranch."

"Now?"

"Yes. Now."

Moments later, he slid open the door to his oldest daughter's room. Tia was asleep but he needed to look at her for himself to see that she was all right. He smiled as he studied her in sleep. She had her mother's mouth, but that was about it. Everything else was his. Her eyes didn't need to be open for him to know they were the exact color of his. A color so rich they looked like dark chocolate.

He'd been the one who'd chosen the name Tia for their first child and it had been Teri's decision to name all the other girls with the starting letter of *T* like his and Teri's names. Tia was determined to follow in her mother's footsteps and become a cowgirl, which was why she'd been taking horse-riding lessons since she turned five. He still didn't like the idea of her competing, though, not even in her age group, which was another thing he and Teri couldn't agree on.

Leaning down, he placed a kiss on Tia's cheek before leaving the room to check on Tatum and Tempest. Both had honey-brown eyes like Teri and favored their mother a lot. There was barely a two-year difference in Tatum's and Tempest's ages and the two were extremely close. They looked out for each other. He liked that about them. He figured that unlike Tia, they would never grow up and ask for separate rooms. They would enjoy being in each other's pockets for as long as they could. Placing kisses on their cheeks, as well, he moved to the room that was closest to his bedroom. The one where three-year-old Tasha slept.

Although he tiptoed into the room, he wasn't surprised when Tasha's eyes flew open and she stared at him a minute before a huge smile touched her lips. "Daddy!"

She threw himself into his arms and he held her. After three girls, he and Teri had been hoping for a boy, but when the nurse had placed Tasha in his arms, it hadn't mattered that he had gotten a fourth girl. Tasha looked more like him than any of the others. She was his Mini-Me.

Picking her up into his arms, he went over to the rocking chair he'd gotten for Tia, the one that had been passed down from daughter to daughter. He gazed down at his daughter and saw dark brown eyes staring back up at him.

"Tasha loves Daddy."

He smiled. "And Daddy loves Tasha."

Cradling her against his chest, he began rocking her back to sleep. Having come back from such a dangerous mission, he needed peace in his life at that moment, but he knew true peace wouldn't come until he went after Teri and found out what was going on with her. Why she'd called his parents to keep the girls so she could get away.

Other than him, his sister and his parents,

Teri had no family. Her parents had died when she was young and her grandparents had raised her on their ranch in Terrell, Texas, which was a stone's throw from Dallas. When Mac had met her, the grandparents she'd adored had died and at twenty-three Teri was trying to run the ranch alone. After their whirlwind romance she'd made the decision—one that he knew had been hard for her, even though she'd never complained about it—to sell the ranch and accept his marriage proposal. She'd turned in her spurs to become a SEAL wife.

It had been her suggestion that they go to a dude ranch for their honeymoon, which would be her last hurrah as a cowgirl. That had been two weeks he'd totally enjoyed, and he'd gotten to show her how well he could handle a horse, thanks to his mother's family, who'd owned a horse ranch in Ocala, Florida.

The timing of their meeting had been perfect. He'd just graduated from the naval academy three years before and was enjoying being a SEAL. It had been his intention to remain a bachelor for quite a while, but all that had changed after he met Teri.

As he continued to rock his daughter back to sleep, Mac closed his eyes, recalling the day Teri Cantor walked into his life...

Ten years ago

"Damn, Lawton, will you slow down?"

Mac glanced over at the man walking beside him. Lawton was walking so fast you'd think he was rushing to put out a fire. Against his better judgment, Mac had let Lawton talk him into coming here of all places—a rodeo—just to see a woman.

"You shouldn't walk so slow," Lawton said, grinning, not breaking his stride.

"Whatever. Now, how did you and this woman meet again?"

"We met online three months ago and officially met last month when I flew to Atlanta for the weekend. She's a photographer for the Bill Pickett Rodeo circuit. LaDorria mentioned they would be in the DC area, so I figured this would be my chance to see her again."

As they neared the entrance to the arena Lawton slowed down and so did Mac. "Is there a particular spot where the two of you plan to meet once we're inside?" Mac asked, looking around.

"Yes. She said to meet her at the booth that sells the commemorative booklets."

Ten minutes later they were there, and Lawton introduced Mac to LaDorria Clark. Mac had to admit she was an attractive woman, and just for the hell of it, he asked if she had a single friend. She quickly replied, "It just so happens I do. Her name is Teri and she's competing tonight."

LaDorria grabbed one of the commemorative booklets and flipped through to a certain page, pointed and said, "This here is Teri."

Mac figured if a man could fall in love with a photograph, then he had done so in that moment. The very beautiful woman in a cowgirl outfit was smiling for the camera and she captured his heart then and there.

"What event is she competing in?"

"Roping and barrel racing. She's the current champ in the women's division. She was also rodeo queen last year."

Mac looked at the photo again. He could definitely believe that. He figured her age was around twenty-two or twenty-three and she had the most gorgeous pair of honey-brown eyes. They were perfect for her high cheekbones and full, shapely lips. Her skin was the color of rich mocha and he loved the way the mass of curly hair fell around her shoulders.

He looked over at LaDorria. "And you'll introduce us?"

She laughed. "Yes, just as soon as the rodeo is over, and only if you cheer for Teri tonight. Like I said, she's competing."

As far as Mac was concerned, Teri Cantor didn't need him cheering for her because she had her own fan section in the stands. And she was good. So good that she won both competitive events easily. He couldn't help admiring how well she handled a horse, how skillfully she rode the animal. Nor could he fight his attraction to her—she was a beautiful woman in person and in action in the ring. And he definitely liked the way she looked in her cowgirl outfits. She had changed into a couple of different ones and each one he would claim as a favorite.

He liked the way she handled a rope and how easily her lasso fell over the cow's head. He knew that sort of aptitude came from hours of practice. That meant she was well disciplined.

Mac had heard the comments from the men around him. Men who'd made it obvious they had the hots for Teri. Some had even admitted to hitting on her and striking out. He hoped he wouldn't be one of those men.

He thought about other women he'd dated in the past. Most liked the idea of dating a military man, but none ever fancied marrying one. They'd all heard the life of a SEAL's wife was too demanding. The thought of not knowing where their husband was and when he'd be returning was just something they couldn't tolerate.

Their attitude was something he hadn't been able to tolerate, either. Although he had no intention of acquiring a wife for years to come, it still bothered him how some women thought a relationship was all about them. They had no idea that a navy SEAL wife was, in a way, serving her country, as well.

"I just got a text from LaDorria," Lawton said at the end of the rodeo. "They asked us to give them thirty minutes and then they'll meet us by that souvenir table again."

"Okay, and it looks like you're kind of serious about LaDorria," he said to Lawton.

"I am. I just hope she's serious about me."

Mac hoped she was, as well, since Lawton was a pretty decent guy.

It was almost forty-five minutes later, but Mac was convinced it was worth every minute of waiting for LaDorria and Teri to arrive. When he saw Teri Cantor walking toward them, he thought she looked even better up close and in person.

She had changed out of her riding outfit into a pair of slacks and a blouse that made her look feminine as hell. Her hair was no longer tied back away from her face but hung in loose curls around her shoulders. He could tell the moment their gazes connected that there was interest between them and he didn't intend to let that interest go to waste.

"So, what do you think?" Lawton leaned over to ask before the two women had approached them.

Mac's response was quick and honest. "I think I'm in love."

Lawton laughed but Mac was totally serious. That was how his father claimed it had been for him when he'd seen Mac's mother for the first time, when the two had been attending classes together at Ohio State University.

Mac drew in a deep breath and didn't release it until the women had reached them. Introductions were being made by LaDorria. "Teri, I'd like you to meet a friend of Lawton's. Thurston McRoy."

Teri offered him her hand and the moment he took it, he felt…something flow through him. From the look in her eyes, he knew she'd felt it, as well.

"Nice meeting you, Thurston."

He smiled down at her. "My friends call me Mac."

She nodded. "Okay. It's nice meeting you, Mac."

"Same here." And he truly meant it.

That night they went to one of the bar-and-grills that stayed open late. He got to know her better but not as well as he wanted to. They exchanged phone numbers and stayed in touch, sometimes talking on the phone at night for hours.

They had their first official date a month later, when he'd flown to Montana to watch her perform in another rodeo. That was when he was about to be stationed in Spain and he'd wanted to see her again before leaving the country.

They exchanged texts and phone calls whenever they could, and it was two months later that she'd told him she was thinking about selling her ranch and moving to New York. She felt that maybe it was time to put her college degree in business to good use. He'd known it would be a tough decision for her to make. From their talks, he knew how much she'd enjoyed living on the ranch.

Once she made the decision to sell the ranch it had sold quickly, and before she could pack up and move to New York, he had persuaded her to visit him in Barcelona. When she said she would, he'd made all the arrangements and had sent her an airline ticket within twenty-four hours. He had been there to pick her up from the airport and the moment he saw her again he'd known he wanted to make her a permanent part of his life.

Teri had spent two wonderful weeks with him in Spain and it was during that time that they'd shared a bed for the first time. Making love to her had been just like he'd known it would be.

She'd literally rocked his world.

The intensity of their sexual joining was powerful. It was as if her body was made for him and his for her.

Before leaving to return to the States, he'd asked her to marry him, and she'd accepted.

A month later they were married.

Bringing his thoughts back to the present, Mac opened his eyes and glanced down at Tasha. She had gone back to sleep. Standing, he placed his daughter back in her bed and then he walked out of the room.

It was time to go find his wife.

Two

Teri McRoy sipped her coffee as she stood at the window and looked out.

For miles all she could see were beautiful plains, valleys and mountains. The Torchlight Dude Ranch, located in Torchlight, Wyoming, was a luxury guest ranch on over a thousand acres just west of Cheyenne. Mac had first brought her here for their honeymoon ten years ago and had promised that one day he would bring her back.

He never had.

Knowing she needed time alone to deal with a few issues, this was the first place she'd thought of coming due to the wonderful and lasting memories she had of the time spent here with Mac. Now she was glad she had come. She missed her girls more than anything and appreciated her in-laws for their quick response in coming to look after them. Her daughters couldn't ask for better grandparents. Mac's parents were the best. She couldn't imagine leaving the girls with anyone else right now. But still, she was compelled to check on them every day. She needed to hear their voices. As expected, they would tell her they missed her—and tell her how much fun they were having with Pop and Nana.

One of the things Teri liked most about this dude ranch was that you didn't have to stay in the main house. If you opted for more privacy, there were several small cabins spread out over the thousand acres. It was beautiful. Part of the package was that you got your very own horse to use daily and it was delivered to you each morning. Hers was a beautiful white stallion named Amsterdam. Over the past three days, she and Amsterdam had gotten to know each other well. She wasn't even put off by his spirited side. Being the horse expert that she was, she loved the challenge.

As she stood there thinking about just how idyllic this cabin was, she knew in her heart the one thing missing was her husband's presence. She missed Mac and always did whenever he was gone for long periods of time, although she tried hard not to let him know it. He had a dangerous job and she'd known that when she had married him. She'd also known he could be summoned away at a moment's notice without being able to inform her of where he was going or how long he'd be gone. The longest time he'd ever been gone was seven months. This time it had been almost nine and she was beginning to worry. What if…

Teri shook her head, refusing to go there. Mac expected her to be strong and handle things while he was gone. Unfortunately, this time around it was hard for her to do that. Things had happened that she hadn't counted on and her heart broke more and more each day.

Mac was a good man. A wonderful father

and loving husband. He provided for his family, whatever their needs were. Financially, Mac's girls didn't want for anything. However, she was discovering that there were some things that money couldn't buy. Peace of mind. More good days than bad. And a marriage that was more blissful than stressful.

A part of her wanted Mac to not only be on the ranch with her to share in the beauty again, but to also just hold her and tell her everything was going to be all right. She needed him to not blame her for what had gone wrong. Even if it was the news of losing the very thing he would have wanted.

A son.

When she felt her tears fall again she drew in a deep breath. Her grief counselor had talked to her, told her that miscarriages were more common than most people even knew. She'd done nothing wrong.

The counselor didn't know the half of it.

She was not supposed to get pregnant. Mac had said that although he would have loved to have a son, when it didn't happen with Tasha that was it. He felt four kids were enough for her to handle on her own while he worked as a SEAL.

They'd talked to her doctor about getting her tubes tied, which could be done as an outpatient procedure. They'd scheduled the surgery, but he'd gotten called away. She was to keep the appointment for the procedure regardless. Then she'd gotten the call from the doctor saying results from presurgical blood work revealed she was already pregnant. There had been no way to reach out to Mac to let him know, but she figured he would eventually be happy about the news. Everything was going fine, but then four months later she'd miscarried.

She fought back the sob rattling her chest. When she was told she was having a boy she'd started thinking of names and in private moments called him TT. Tiny Thurston. She had wanted to share the news with Mac and had worried that by the time he returned, she would have had their son without him.

Wiping the tears from her eyes, she finished the rest of the coffee before forcing her mind to remember something else…namely that phone

call she had received from the man who'd been
her grandparents' attorney and the news he'd
given her. The couple she'd sold her ranch to,
close to twelve years ago now, were putting it
on the market. According to the terms of the
contract, they had to give her the first opportunity to buy it back. At the time she'd made
that stipulation, she didn't think they would go
for it, but the Jacobins had wanted to buy the
ranch badly enough to agree with her terms.
And of course, she'd thought they would never
sell the ranch, but according to her grandparents' former attorney, because of Mr. Jacobin's
failing health, they had no choice.

For her, that offer was a dream come true.
She'd only been given ten days to take it and
it had to be done in person. Unlike when
she'd sold the ranch, she and Mac now had
the means to buy it back. But the time frame
meant the decision had to be made without
Mac's input. So, she had.

She had weighed the advantages against the
disadvantages and, in the end, she'd decided
that buying the ranch would be good for her
family. A bigger house. More land for their

kids to spread out and enjoy. Getting back to nature. A way to supplement their income after Mac retired, if they decided to raise cattle for market.

Remembering her days spent on the ranch while growing up, she wanted the same kind of memories for her girls. There were good schools in the area and although most of the neighbors who'd been her grandparents' friends had passed on, their heirs were people Teri had grown up with and whom she looked forward to sharing friendships with again.

Teri had figured she wouldn't be gone but for a day and appreciated her neighbor and friend Carla for agreeing to watch the kids while Teri flew to Terrell, Texas, to finalize the sale. The day after she returned to Virginia was when she began having stomach pains. Within twenty-four hours, she'd lost the baby. Although the doctor claimed her traveling had nothing to do with it, she couldn't help wondering if it had.

She'd gained the ranch she'd thought lost to her for good, but lost the baby she'd never expected to have.

Losing the baby had been hard and she appreciated her in-laws for their love and support during a very difficult time for her. She'd tried pulling herself out of the slump she'd felt herself slowly sinking into, and when she'd been nearly at her wit's end, she'd called her in-laws after her grief counselor suggested she get away for a while.

Had the home she'd repurchased been empty she would have gone there, but the sellers had asked to remain in the house three months before they were required to move out. She had no problem with that since Mac was gone on a mission and she didn't want to move their family to the ranch without letting him know what she'd done. She could just imagine Mac returning home to find a for sale sign on their home in Virginia without knowing all the details of why.

So here she was trying to deal with a number of things and wishing her husband was here with her. But then, maybe it was a good thing he wasn't. She believed he would understand how she felt about losing the baby and give her all the support and love she needed, but there was also the issue of the ranch she'd purchased. Would he understand that she'd done what she felt she had to do in the time limit she'd been given? They'd talked about getting a new house, but how would he feel about moving from Virginia to Texas? To the house that used to be her childhood home?

The other piece was that she'd paid a lot for the purchase, deciding to pay cash instead of getting a mortgage. How would Mac react when he found out she'd used their money to do so, without consulting him?

All those questions with no answers were issues that had kept her up at night.

She had endured long weeks of foreboding and her senses were filled with unease and worry about both situations. The surgery to have her tubes tied had been rescheduled and she was having apprehensions about that, and although a part of her wanted to believe that buying the ranch had been for the best, she wasn't sure how Mac would feel about it.

Being here at *this* ranch had helped soothe

her mind and she didn't regret coming here, although she did miss the girls. There were so many activities to enjoy, and yesterday she'd even helped with the branding of the cattle and participated in a roundup. After today, she would only have four days left here and then she would return to Virginia, to her daughters and to wait for Mac to come home.

Mac.

Lately things hadn't been so great between them.

They seemed to argue more when he returned after being away. She didn't think it was related to PTSD; it was just a case of two strong-willed individuals not always agreeing on certain things. It was so hard for him to understand that while he was away, she was both mom and dad, and when he returned it wasn't easy for her to relinquish one of them. Usually by the time she did, he was gone again. Why was it becoming a vicious cycle that seemed to threaten their marriage to the point where she'd begun feeling that she was taken for granted?

There it was again.

Questions with no answers. Problems that needed solving.

She wanted, for the time being, to clear her mind of all of it and to recall a time when she didn't have any worries. Or at least not too many—for even back then she had been trying to decide how she would run a ranch without her grandparents. But all those years ago she had been a young girl who'd met a man she knew was meant to be a part of her life and she a part of his.

As she stood there sipping her coffee, her mind drifted back to that time…

Ten years ago

Less than an hour after her friend LaDorria had introduced them, Teri had known Thurston McRoy was a take-charge kind of man who was military through and through.

In addition to being breathtakingly handsome, he was also incredibly charming and outrageously kind. She'd discovered just how kind when they'd left the rodeo and they'd gone, along with LaDorria and Lawton, to this bar-and-grill for food and beer. He'd opened doors for her, pulled out chairs and hadn't tried taking control of their conversations.

He hadn't come on too strong, yet he'd managed to overwhelm her just the same. She had discovered he was someone easy to talk to, someone who had the ability to make her feel comfortable around him. It seemed LaDorria and Lawton had intentionally left them alone by staying on the dance floor. But she hadn't minded. It was during that time that she'd gotten to size him up. To see how he treated people, from the waiter who took their order to the busboy who'd come to clear off their table. He'd treated everyone with respect and gone out of his way to make their servers feel appreciated.

Although she had enjoyed that night with Mac, she hadn't been certain he would want to see her again. He'd asked for her phone number at the end of the night, but that didn't particularly mean anything. She'd long discovered that some men didn't care about dating a girl who not only loved horses but who was an ace on the back of one. Then there was her skill with a rope and her expertise with barrel racing. They preferred women who were all class and sophistication. Ones who wore expensive gowns rather than jeans and a Western shirt.

It didn't take long for her to see Mac wasn't that type of man. He had followed up their date with a number of phone calls. Her ability to rope a calf didn't bother him and he'd even said he liked how she looked in a pair of jeans. He'd told her that although he wasn't an expert on a horse like she was, he could ride and enjoyed riding because his grandparents owned a horse ranch.

Then there was the night he'd surprised her and shown up at one of her rodeos in Montana. She had won her competition that night and had felt good about it. After the rodeo she had seen him waiting on her, dressed as a cowboy with a Stetson on his head. She had found herself even more attracted to him and had offered no resistance when he'd taken her hand to lead her over to the SUV he'd rented.

"Where are we going?" she asked him when he opened the vehicle's door.

"I'm taking you somewhere to celebrate

your win. You looked fantastic out there and you did an awesome job."

His words had made her feel good. Pretty darn special and she felt even more special in his company.

They'd had a lively discussion on their way to the restaurant for dinner. He'd told her more about both his grandfathers and how their time in the military had made him desire a military life of his own. She knew when his maternal grandfather had retired he and Mac's grand-mother had purchased a ranch in Florida.

"I've never been to Florida."

He glanced over at her strangely when he brought the car to a stop in the restaurant's parking lot. "You haven't?"

"No. I heard the beaches there are beautiful."

He nodded. "They are, but then, Texas has beautiful beaches. I remember spending the weekend in Galveston one year."

She'd been tempted to inquire who he'd spent the weekend with but hadn't. Instead she said, "I bet you had a lot of fun."

"I did," he said, grinning over at her.

During the walk to the restaurant's door he

told her more about himself and the more she got to know about him, the more she liked him. That night had pretty much established how things would be between them. She had accepted that he'd opted for a career as a navy SEAL and she knew any woman in his life would have to live with that choice. Since she'd been seriously considering selling her ranch, the idea of having a life with him, which would include traveling around the world, intrigued her.

When he invited her to Barcelona, she'd said yes right away, and those two weeks had been a game changer. She'd seen just what life with Mac would be like. As he showed her around Spain, she'd fallen in love with him. She had been a virgin and the night they'd made love for the first time was something she would never forget. He had made it special for her.

They had talked a lot, as well. Mac had told about his parents' interracial marriage and how dedicated they'd been to making it successful, remaining partners in all things. That was the kind of marriage he wanted for himself. One filled with love and commitment.

She'd known that was the kind of marriage she wanted for herself, too, one where divorce would never be an option. The kind she was raised to believe her own parents had found, and the kind she knew her grandparents had shared.

Those had been the best two weeks of her life and before she left to return to the United States, he'd asked her to marry him.

Not seeing any reason to have a long engagement, they'd gotten married a month later and she had no regrets.

Teri brought her thoughts back to the present. Lawton and LaDorria had gotten married a year after Mac and Teri and they were still together, living in New Mexico with their two kids. Lawton had gotten out of the military and had gone to work for the FBI. LaDorria had expanded her love of photography and opened her own shop. Teri and Mac heard from them from time to time, and she always looked forward to the Christmas photo card they sent each year. They always looked so happy. So perfect. She didn't want to think about how things weren't so photo perfect with her and Mac.

Placing the coffee cup aside, she moved toward the bedroom. It was time to get dressed for her daily morning ride on Amsterdam.

"I'm sorry, Mr. McRoy, but your name is not on the registration. Until Mrs. McRoy gives her permission for you to be added, we can't give you a key to her cabin."

Mac forced back his anger, trying to understand the man's position. He knew the rules were due to security measures, which he should appreciate. After all, for all the staff knew, he could very well be an ex-husband intent on doing bodily harm to his wife. That wasn't the case, although he would admit his anger had only grown on the flight here. It had been his fifth flight in less than twenty-four hours. His fifth flight since his commanding officer had told the team they were free to go home and, unless there was some type of international crisis that required their SEAL team to go into action, they had the next six months on leave.

It was six months all of them needed after their last operation. Because of the success of their mission, Americans would be able to sleep safe at night, and to him and his teammates, that was what truly mattered. But for him the battle wasn't over whenever he returned home. Those were the times he had to fight to reconnect with Teri. "That's fine," he finally said, seeing the man's features relax. He knew the clerk had expected an argument and a part of Mac was raring to give him one, but what would have been the use? "Do you have any idea where she is so she can give me permission?"

"We tried calling the cabin and she's not answering, so we can only assume she's out riding. I believe she does that every morning."

"Does she come here for breakfast?"

"No. She's in one of the cabins farthest away, one with a stocked kitchen." And then, as if realizing he might have provided too much information, he added, "That's all I can tell you. I left Ms. McRoy a voice-mail message. If you'd like to sit over there and wait, I'm sure she will be returning my call shortly."

"I'd rather wait outside. That way I can walk around a bit to stretch my legs. Can I leave my gear here while I do?"

"Yes, sir, you can."

Mac handed his duffel bag to the man before turning to walk out the door. He stepped out on the porch and drew in a deep breath, appreciating the moment of breathing in good American air. He'd been in Libya too long and was glad to be home. Only thing, he wasn't home. It wasn't even close enough to home to suit him. Getting on another plane within a few hours after getting off one hadn't made his day or his night, which he was yet to have. He hadn't slept in over thirty hours.

Glancing around, he saw the changes that had been made since the last time he'd been here on his honeymoon. There was a spanking new barn that was a lot bigger than the last one had been. Even the main ranch house had gotten a face-lift. It was three times the size it was before. He'd noticed the sign that read Under New Management the moment he'd walked into the place.

He was about to step off the porch when his

cell phone rang. Recognizing the ringtone, he pulled the phone out of the back pocket of his jeans and clicked on. "Yeah, Bane?"

"You know the routine, Mac. You didn't touch base with any of us to let us know you'd gotten home."

He released a frustrated breath before saying, "I'm not home."

"Why the hell not?" That question came from another team member, Gavin Blake, whose code name was Viper. That meant in addition to Viper and Bane, Mac was on a call with the other two team members he was close friends with, as well: David Holloway, whose code name was Flipper, and Laramie Cooper, whose code name was Coop.

"Because when I got home, I discovered Teri was missing."

"Missing? What do you mean Teri was missing?" Flipper wanted to know.

"And your answer better be good, Mac. I hope she hasn't finally taken enough of your BS and left your ass," Coop added.

Mac rubbed his hand down his face. He didn't need his teammates to remind him that at times he wasn't the easiest man to get along with. "Will the four of you calm down?" Leaning against the porch post, he then told them what he knew. At least what his parents had told him. Which hadn't been much.

"And you haven't seen her yet?" Bane asked.

"No. I haven't been here but a few minutes. She's out riding and since my name isn't on her registration, they won't tell me which cabin she's staying in or give me a key."

"That's understandable," Viper said.

"Yes, but that doesn't mean I have to like it."

"Calm down, Mac," Bane warned.

Now they were the ones telling him to calm down. "I am calm. I haven't hit anything yet."

"And you won't. Listen to what Teri has to say. She must have had a good reason for taking off and leaving the kids with your folks," Coop was saying.

"Yes, and try to be understanding, no matter the reason," Viper suggested.

"And another thing," Flipper, the most recently married one of the team, spoke up to say, but Mac stopped him.

"Hold up. I don't need you guys giving me

marital advice. I've been married a lot longer than any of you."

"That might be true, but you have a tendency to act like an ass at times, like you know everything," Coop said. "We've been gone awhile. Eight months, twelve days and fifteen hours to be exact. Show your woman how much you miss her, love her and appreciate her."

Mac shook his head. "Like I said, guys, I don't need your advice. I know how to handle my business."

"Your way of handling things doesn't work all the time, Mac," Viper said. "That's all we're saying."

Mac rubbed the back of his neck and felt a tension headache coming on. He never got headaches. "Duly noted. Now, goodbye."

"Hey, call us later to let us know things are okay," Bane said.

Mac rolled his eyes. "I'll think about it." He then clicked off the phone.

Teri had returned to the cabin after her morning ride and was about to go into the

kitchen to prepare something to eat for breakfast when she noticed the blinking light on the
cabin's telephone. She thought about ignoring
it, thinking it was probably the resort man-
ager giving her a rundown of that day's activities. However, she felt compelled to answer it
anyway. Her cell phone was out of range and
wasn't working. What if it was her in-laws
trying to reach her?

Moving quickly to the phone, she picked it
up to retrieve the message. "Ms. McRoy, this
is Harold at the front desk. Please call me as
soon as you get this message."

Teri pressed the number seven and Harold
picked up immediately. "Harold, you called.
Is something wrong?"

"No, ma'am. There's a man here who says
he's your husband and has asked for a key to
your cabin. Company policy restricts us from
doing that. Said his name is Thurston McRoy."

Teri's heart suddenly began pounding hard
in her chest. Mac was here? She drew in a
deep breath. He must have returned and found
she'd left and her in-laws had told him where

she was? Had they also told him why she'd taken off? Did he know—

"Ms. McRoy? Is it okay to give him a key with directions on how to get to your cabin?"

She swallowed. "Is he there? If so, please let me talk with him."

"No, he's not here inside. He stepped outside."

Probably to cool off, she thought. Coming home and finding her gone had probably pissed him off. Coming after her would have made him angrier. Then being denied access to her cabin would have made the situation even worse.

"I can go outside and get him if you need to talk to him."

She drew in a deep breath. Knowing Mac, she figured that would agitate him even more. "No, that's not necessary. Please give him a key and directions on how to get here."

"Okay, I will."

When Teri hung up the phone, she drew in a deep breath.

She wouldn't have those additional three days alone here after all.

Three

Mac saw Teri the moment the SUV rounded a corner off a battered road lined with oak trees. It was in a secluded area and he wasn't sure he liked knowing she'd gotten a cabin so far from the main house. He didn't care one iota that the front desk guy had said someone from the office checked on her and all the other cabins every morning when they brought the horses.

She was dressed in Western attire and leaning against a post on a small porch. She looked good in a pair of jeans that fit perfectly over her curves, a long-sleeved shirt that, to his way of thinking, looked a little too snug over what he knew were beautiful breasts. A pair of riding boots were on her feet and a hat was covering that mass of gorgeous hair on her head.

It had been eight months since he'd seen her and at that moment his eyes couldn't help but drink in the sight of her. Damn. He'd missed her. She looked good but he couldn't let her looks and how deeply she'd been missed sway how upset he was with her right now. She owed him an explanation.

But still…

He couldn't help the flutter he felt in his heart or the yearning he felt in his soul. They might have their disagreements, some worse than others, but he knew he loved her. Always had and always would. He then thought about those disagreements. Lately there had been a lot of them. Too many. His teammates were right about him and his attitude. He tried working on it every time he returned home but Teri had a knack for making wild decisions about too many things at a time. He always looked at the whole picture. She didn't. If it was something she wanted, then she would find a way to justify them getting it. Then she would go on the defensive when he questioned her about it.

Mac didn't have a problem with her spending money—he just needed her to do so wisely. He remembered his parents' struggles over money and had sworn when he became an adult that wouldn't be him. Of course later he learned most of their struggles had been about sacrifices they'd made for him and Kylie.

Although his parents were pretty close to their own parents, during the earlier years of their marriage, neither liked hitting them up for loans when they'd encountered financial challenges. That wasn't the McRoy way. They had taught him early in life that if you make the bills, then you were responsible for paying them. That's one of the reasons he'd learned early to invest his money and had a nice bank account when he'd married Teri. He'd been intent on making sure she got all the things she needed, but not necessarily those things she wanted just for the sake of having them. There should always be money for rainy days, and then he was also focused on generational wealth to pass on to his daughters. Something his parents hadn't been able to do for him or his sister. So far the stock market had been good and those investments were better than he'd ever imagined.

Bringing the SUV to a stop in front of the cabin, he cut the ignition. She hadn't moved. She was still standing there, leaning against the post with one of those "I need to decipher your mood before I approach" looks on her face. Whether she knew it or not, usually that look told him more than what he wanted to know. Now he couldn't help wondering just what had gone on while he'd been away. He was also curious about how she had handled it and whether or not he would agree with the outcome.

He got out of the vehicle and closed the door behind him. "Teri." He suddenly felt his gut clench from the effect her honey-brown eyes had on him.

"Hi, Mac."

He tried not to focus on her lips but was powerless to do anything less. He loved her lips. The shape. The taste. And then because neither of them could help themselves after being separated for over eight months, they began moving toward each other as sexual tension sizzled between them. The moment she was there, standing directly in front of him, he pulled her into his arms. Explanations would come later. Right now, this was what he needed. The feel of her warm, feminine body pressed against his and the taste of her mouth.

He kissed her, long and deep, the woman he'd loved for over ten years. The woman who had rocked his world the first time he'd seen her. The woman who still managed to remind him what a damn lucky bastard he was even on those days when he felt like nothing was going right with her. She was the mother of his children and the reason he fought hard during every covert operation. He wanted to come back to her.

To this.

He deepened the kiss and she reciprocated in kind. He loved her taste. Always had and he figured he always would. She moaned into his mouth and he loved the sound. It had been a while since the last time he'd heard it. And he wanted more. More moans. More of her body pressed against his. He wanted her naked.

She could explain the reason she'd felt the need to come here later. He needed her now.

Sweeping her off her feet, he carried her into the house.

Teri felt them moving and knew they were headed for the bedroom. She had to stop him. More important, she had to stop herself from once again being totally overwhelmed by Mac. She wanted him and he wanted her and, in the past, knowing that had been enough.

But not this time.

She was tired of the off-the-chart-lovemaking followed by the questions and arguments. They needed to talk first.

When she yanked her mouth from his, he placed her on her feet, and she scrambled out of his arms. She looked up at him. Mac was tall, way over six feet. He had skin the color of café au lait, dark brown eyes, solid cheekbones, a sturdy neck and a pair of the sexiest lips any man had a right to own. And whether he was clean-shaven or sporting a beard on his masculine jaw like he was doing now, Mac was a hunk. A very sensuous and handsome hunk. He stood there, his focus entirely on her, and the desire she saw in his eyes wasn't helping the situation.

"What's wrong, Teri?"

If only he knew.

"We need to talk first, Mac." She needed to tell him everything. About the baby and about the purchase of her ranch. Not to mention all the doubts she'd been having.

He reached back out for her. "We can talk later."

That was his answer for almost everything. Whenever sexual need took over his mind on his return from a mission, the lovemaking would come first, followed by a good whole day of sleep. After that he'd spend quality time with the girls. Only then would he turn his well-rested, all-too-critical attention to her. He would ask how things had gone while he'd been away. She would tell him. Then the arguments would start. He would tell her how he would have handled the situation differently had he been there.

That "I know what's best" attitude would rattle her. It was what had driven them to seek marriage counseling when they'd reached the five-year mark in their marriage. He'd disliked Mr. Blum, the counselor. He hadn't like airing their dirty laundry to a total stranger, nor had he liked having that same person remind him that marriage was a partnership.

"No, Mac, we need to talk now."

He eyed her warily. "Why can't it hold, baby? I missed you. I love you and I need you, Teri. I need you bad."

She drew in a deep breath, knowing that was that. Those sentences got to her as much as the sight of him standing there.

Her Mac.

Because she knew from the look in his eyes that he did need her. She never knew what happened during those covert operations, the hell he went through, or how close he came to losing his life. Any information was highly classified and he couldn't tell her, so he held it inside. But she would know how hard it had been from the intensity of their lovemaking whenever he returned. And his words were always the key. The words he'd just spoken pretty much let her know that before they talked, he felt an urgency to let himself go. To reclaim his soul and hold on to his sanity. He wanted to forget all the anguish of the last eight months. Forget it and release it in her arms.

But what about her anguish? Wanting to reclaim her soul and hold on to her sanity? What about how she'd suffered in losing the baby she'd wanted and how she inwardly blamed herself…no matter what the doctor said. She would always wonder if traveling to Texas had been the cause.

"Teri?"

Mac saying her name made her realize that she'd just been standing there, staring at him. He had extended his hand out to her. Should she take it and find peace in his arms for a little while? Could they put off talking for later like he'd suggested?

Knowing no matter how much she wanted to, probably should, she couldn't deny Mac anything.

At that moment he was as crucial to her as she believed she was to him.

She took the couple of steps to him and placed her hand in his. He pulled her closer and swept her back into his arms to carry her into the bedroom.

When he placed her on the bed, at that moment everything felt good, right, so totally perfect. For now, she would put out of her mind any thoughts of those things that had driven her here. Instead she would give her full concentration to the man whose eyes were connected to hers. The man who was looking at her with intense, deep passion and desire.

And she was returning that gaze with the same need and longing. She knew her eyes were filled with the desire of a woman who loved and appreciated the man standing beside the bed, staring down at her. He'd removed his shirt and she thought the same thing now that she had when they'd met over ten years ago. Thurston McRoy was a very good-looking man. The six-foot-three-inch hulk of a navy SEAL could be one tough-as-nails badass but also a total pushover when it came to his girls.

Although she might not know the details of the covert operation he'd just left, there was no doubt he and his teammates had been through hell and back and that they had left their mark on anyone who dared to threaten the country they loved.

"Like what you see, Teri Anne?"

He always asked her that question and her response would always be the same. Yes, she loved what she saw, especially his well-built body. He exercised often, and it showed. He was slightly older than most of his teammates and claimed he had to make sure he stayed in shape to keep up with them. Whatever the reason, he wore his age of thirty-nine well. She wondered if he was still thinking of retiring from military service at forty-one. He hadn't talked about retirement much lately. Her husband was a SEAL through and through and she couldn't imagine him being anything else. A lot of people assumed SEALs were paid a huge salary for the risks they took with their lives for their country, but they weren't. Most made under sixty thousand a year. She knew for most military men it wasn't about the salary but the service. She could say the same for Mac. The only reason they had everything they needed was because of his initiative in investing alongside his friend Bane Westmoreland.

Knowing he was still waiting on her response, she said, "Yes, I definitely like what I see, Thurston McRoy."

She mostly referred to him by his given name in the bedroom. She called him Thurston and he called her Teri Anne. They felt doing so created an even more intimate bond between them. Like they were using that time to not only deepen their connection but to get to know each other all over again. Something they felt they needed to do whenever he returned from his long excursions.

Smiling, he leaned down and captured her lips and she suddenly became drenched in passion of the most provocative kind. Eight months was a long time to be without each other and their bodies were letting them know it. The starvation and greed were evident.

Their tongues tangled and swirled, feasting on each other. For a minute it was hard to decipher which one was his and which was hers. Didn't matter. They shared the hunger, the persistence, the ravenousness. Everything about Mac was delectable—his taste, the way she fit in his arms, the way their bodies meshed together like that was the way they were supposed to be.

Finally, he snatched his mouth back and began undressing her with the urgency of a man who knew what he wanted but thought he might just die before getting it. When she was totally naked, he paused a moment and stared at her with the keen eyes of a husband. A lover. A man who knew her body in and out. Could he detect that something had been there that he hadn't known about? But was there no more?

"You're beautiful as ever. I am one hell of a lucky man."

His words made a knot in her throat thicken. He could say some of the most touching things. "And I'm a lucky woman."

Her head began whirling as he lowered his mouth to hers again and captured her mouth like he had before. Like he had every right to do so and intended to take full advantage of that fact.

Breaking off the kiss he moved back to remove the rest of his clothes and she got turned on just watching him. Jeans so tight they seemed imprinted on his flesh were slid down tight, masculine thighs. Then he stood there in sexy black briefs that clearly defined how well-endowed her man was.

Her man.

Yes, he was that and he would continue to be her man. Whatever issues they were dealing with were merely hiccups along the way. They would just have to deal with them later. She just hoped that when they did, they would remember this time when they pushed all thoughts, except for each other, aside, and put their love front and center.

She watched him ease his briefs down his legs and then he moved toward her with blazing hot desire burning in his eyes. "I want you," she whispered.

"I want you, too," he whispered back, placing a knee on the bed and then drawing her to him. He kissed her again, long and deep, before releasing her and moving back from the bed to stare at her nakedness.

She felt her stomach tighten and her navel tingle. Seeing him without clothes was making heat consume her from top to bottom. "I love undressing you. I've thought of doing it every single day I was gone."

His words sparked every cell within her. Mac had the ability to use words to take her to another level. That, combined with her physical attraction to him and the sexual chemistry that always seemed to radiate between them, made what they were sharing mind-blowingly extraordinary. The thought that he could desire her so deeply always did something to her.

He moved back to the bed and whispered erotic words in several different languages as he lowered her back against the pillows. And when he towered over her, she felt overwhelmed by the look she saw in his eyes.

She felt his hard shaft sliding inside her and she cried out his name, loving the feel of him stretching her. He kept going deep until he couldn't go any more. He began moving, slow at first, then faster, thrusting in and out, and she couldn't help crying out his name again and again. Then a climax struck her, ripping through her with an impact that nearly stopped her breathing.

She heard Mac's deep growl, the prologue to his orgasmic release. His thrusts kept coming, deeper and harder, and then she felt the instant his body began trembling above her, exploding inside of her.

"Teri…" He whispered her name seconds before leaning in and taking her mouth in his, kissing her as if to make up for the eight months they'd been apart.

She returned his kiss with just as much hunger and need. When he finally released her mouth she whispered, "Welcome back, Mac."

Then he reclaimed her mouth as if to start their lovemaking process all over again.

Four

Teri raced Amsterdam across the grassy plains with her hair blowing in the wind.

She loved this and hadn't realized how much she'd missed racing until this trip. With Tia taking riding classes, Teri had saddled up to ride, as well. But racing her horse was what she liked best. She needed this and she needed it now.

She had awakened that morning feeling somewhat dazed after making love to her husband most of yesterday and last night. Her pulse pounded every time she thought of all the things they'd done. At one point she'd thought he had fallen asleep from exhaustion and she had moved to ease out of bed.

Mac had awakened quickly and looked over at her. His eyes, laden with sleep, still managed to simmer with desire, and he had then proceeded to show her once again just how badly he wanted her.

She didn't have to go into town to call to check on the kids. Although her cell phone didn't work, Mac's special government issue security phone worked just fine. They'd talked to Mac's parents and the girls.

Late yesterday evening they had left the cabin to drive to Cheyenne for dinner and to shop at one of the Western outfitters. Mac had told her he would be staying with her for the rest of the week, which she'd figured he would. He had purchased several pieces of Western wear and he looked sexy as hell wearing a Stetson on his head.

She figured they would get the chance to have their talk during dinner but instead he steered the conversation, deliberately or otherwise, to other things. Such as the monstrosity of a house his teammate Bane Westmoreland

and his wife, Crystal, were having built. They would be hosting a housewarming party when the house was completed and Mac and Teri were invited to attend.

She'd followed his line of conversation and brought him up to date on the girls, telling him how well Tia was doing with her horse-riding lessons and how Tatum had expressed an interest in gymnastics. And of course that meant Tempest was interested, too. She'd mentioned how she'd called in a plumber for the kitchen sink and about their yardman's illness. He'd listened as he always did and asked questions when he'd needed to do so.

She slowed Amsterdam down and headed back toward the cabin. This was the second time she'd ridden him today. As Mac usually did after returning from a long operation, he had slept through breakfast and lunch and there was no reason not to think he wouldn't sleep through dinner. He always said it was only when he was back on American soil he could let his guard down and sleep peacefully. Usually the girls, upon hearing their father had returned home, would camp outside the bedroom door waiting for him to wake up. He had a close relationship with their daughters and was a good dad.

As she trotted the horse back toward the cabin, she saw Mac. He was standing in the same spot on the porch where she'd been standing yesterday when he had arrived. He was leaning against the post, jeans riding low on his hips, shirtless and with a Stetson on his head.

She tightened her hands on the horse's reins. Her libido should be exhausted after the sexual activities she and Mac had participated in during the past twenty-four hours. Instead, however, it was flaring back to life. Why did he have to look so sexy standing there while sipping his coffee with his full attention on her?

She brought the horse to a stop and eased down, tying Amsterdam to the hitching post. "You're up, I see."

"Yes, and the first thing I noticed was that you were gone."

She came up the steps to him. "Did you honestly expect me to stay in bed and sleep as long as you did?"

"You used to."

She nodded, remembering. Yes, she had. That was before their first child. Whenever he came back from being gone on one of his operations, she'd been more than happy to spend her time lying in bed beside him for hours, days and nights.

She tilted her head back to look up at him. "That was the pre-babies days."

He chuckled. "You're right about that. In fact, I do believe it was during one of those sleep-ins that Tia was conceived."

It had been and him bringing that up reminded her of the reason she'd come to the dude ranch in the first place. "Yes, that's when Tia was conceived."

Neither one of them said anything for a minute and then Mac said, "I think it's time for us to talk, Teri. I need to know what drove you to come here."

As far as she was concerned it was past time. "Okay, let's talk."

She walked past him to go inside and he followed.

* * *

Mac watched his wife dust herself off before sitting down on the sofa. "Let me put this away," he said, before going into the kitchen to place the empty coffee cup in the sink.

She had wanted to tell him yesterday about whatever had driven her here and he should have been ready to hear it then. After all, he'd come home to find her gone, with his parents suddenly developing lockjaw about why she'd taken off. During the flight here, he'd been antsy about hearing what she had to say.

Then he'd seen her and the only thing he'd wanted was her. That had been pretty damn understandable since she was his wife and he hadn't seen or touched her in eight months. Teri would always be a desirable woman to him. In reality, she was a lot more. Whether she knew it or not, she was his life. He loved her so damn much. His teammates thought if she didn't know her value to him it was his damn fault for not telling her and saying it often.

Mac always felt he shouldn't have to tell her because she should know that she and the girls meant everything to him. He didn't take any chances with his life because of them. His goal for every covert operation was to come home alive and in one piece to Teri and the girls. He loved being a husband and father.

Returning to the living room, he took the seat across from her. It didn't take a rocket scientist to see that she was nervous. Why?

"So what is it, Teri? What big-ticket item did you buy while I was gone that was over-the-top enough to send you here?"

He could tell by the surprised look on her face that he'd been right. She had bought something and whatever it was, she knew it would be something he wouldn't like. Last year it had been a new bedroom set when they'd given Tia their old one. That didn't bother him as much as the price she'd paid for it. As far as he was concerned, a bed that cost that much should have the ability to sing them to sleep. They didn't have to worry about making ends meet, but it was the principle!

"That's not the reason I came here, Mac."

He nodded. "Okay, then, what's the reason?"

For a long moment, she didn't say anything

and he watched her intently. When he saw the first sign of the tears that appeared in her eyes, he was out of his chair in a flash. He went over to the sofa and pulled her into his arms. His wife wasn't a crier unless she was truly upset about something.

"What is it, Teri? What's wrong?"

She looked up at him and took a deep breath, as if trying to find the courage to tell him whatever she had to say. He tensed, not knowing what would come next, and hoped he was prepared for whatever it was.

"We agreed that we wouldn't have any more children, and I was to have that surgery."

He watched her closely. "Yes, we did agree to that. I wanted to be here with you for the surgery, but then I got that call from my commanding officer to leave immediately. You said you would have the surgery as scheduled and get the folks to come help out with the kids."

Mac watched her features and had an idea where this conversation was headed. "Are you trying to tell me that you didn't have the surgery after all, Teri?" He'd known that although they'd agreed the surgery was necessary, having another child would not have bothered her in the least.

"I couldn't."

He stared at her. "What do you mean you couldn't? We agreed that you would."

"I know, but—"

"Let me guess," he interrupted to say. "You changed your mind about having it done, right? It wouldn't be the first time you reneged on something we agreed to do, Teri. You had no right to take it upon yourself to do that. That was a decision we'd made together."

She pushed out of his arms, her features furious. "Damn you, Mac, don't you think I know what we agreed to do. I was going to have the procedure done, but like I said, I couldn't," she said, almost screaming at him, clearly getting emotional.

"Why?" he asked, crossing his arms over his chest.

"Because when I had my presurgical workup done, the doctor discovered I was pregnant."

Mac's head began spinning. He dropped his arms to his side. "Pregnant?"

"Yes, pregnant! Although a baby was something we hadn't planned, I figured you would want him."

"Him?"

"Yes, him. I carried our son for four months and then I lost him. I lost my baby. Our baby." She then rushed from the house.

He stood there in shock. Teri had been pregnant? She'd gotten as far as four months and then miscarried? Their son? Oh, my God, what had happened? Snapping out of his shock, he quickly went to the door after her. He opened it in time to see Teri galloping off on that horse.

Teri kept riding, refusing to look back when Mac called after her and rebuffing the idea of going back to finish her conversation with him. At the moment she needed to get as far away as she could in order to pull herself together. Then she would go back. But not now.

She needed to be alone.

She knew Mac and truly believed that although they hadn't planned for a baby, he would have wanted their son. It would not have mattered if it had been a boy or girl. Mac would have wanted their baby. He loved kids. They both did. They had wanted three but had decided to try a fourth time for a boy. When it turned out to be a girl, they'd decided to have no more tries and had agreed four was enough.

Teri knew the only reason Mac had gone off like he had just now was because they were still at odds with each other. He believed she would defy him at every turn, and unfortunately, over the years, she had given him reason to think so. She never did anything deliberately, but it always seemed that way to him.

What he had to understand and what she'd tried explaining to him countless times was that when he was gone, she became the head of the household. That meant she had to make decisions without him. He claimed he didn't have a problem with that, yet he never agreed with any of the choices she made.

He would return home and begin questioning her decisions. On top of that he tried to control everything, as if he could just reappear after being gone for months and disrupt their lives. While he was gone, everything ran like a finely tuned machine. When he returned, that machine would break down. He would be so glad to see the girls that he would let them get away with murder. Then when he left it was up to her to implement martial law all over again and become what the girls thought of as the mean parent. She was sick and tired of him questioning what she did and why she did it. She wanted a marriage where she felt any decision she made wouldn't be questioned and ridiculed.

She slowed Amsterdam down to a trot and noticed she was in a different area from where she'd ridden before. Ahead she saw a large windmill and remembered that when they'd come here for their honeymoon this had been a coal miners' camp. Several mines were in the area and were now deserted, their openings boarded up.

Teri had been a history major in college and recalled that years ago several settlements in Wyoming had been considered mining towns. Even now Wyoming was the largest producer of coal in the country. She wondered when these particular mines had shut down since she recalled them being in operation when she'd been here on her honeymoon.

She nudged Amsterdam toward an area where she'd seen a huge lake the first day she'd ridden out this far. That particular area had reminded her of a section of her grandparents' property, which was now legally hers again. She wished she could be happy about that but knew she couldn't until she told Mac what she'd done.

It didn't take her long to reach the lake. Getting off Amsterdam, she tied him to a tree and decided to walk around awhile to calm her nerves before heading back. Before knowing all the facts, Mac had reacted pretty angrily to her not having that procedure done. If his reaction was an example of his mood, she wasn't in any hurry to tell him about her ranch. But she would tell him. It was best to tell him everything, let him get mad and then get over it.

And he would get over it, eventually.

She just hated this pattern they had to go through whenever he returned home. Should they seek marriage counseling again? She knew that was out of the question since he'd hated it the last time. Still, Teri couldn't discount the potential of another issue being added to the mix. Like she'd told him, she hadn't gotten that surgical procedure done. What she hadn't told him was that she hadn't been taking any type of birth control since. His arrival had been unexpected and when they'd made love, he hadn't used protection. What if she was pregnant again? Had he considered that possibility yet? Would he understand why she still hadn't gotten the procedure done three months later?

No, he wouldn't understand.

The more she thought about it, the more she felt she still needed time to herself. She'd told him what had happened with the baby and for now that was enough. At a later time she would go more into details, but for now she needed her time here to deal with things without him. The best way to handle Mac was to ask him to leave.

She wasn't sure how long she'd walked around the lake, deep in her thoughts, when suddenly she heard the sound of a horse approaching. When she glanced around, she saw it was Mac. He was racing his horse toward her. Unsurprisingly, he had a fierce frown on his face.

He barely brought the horse to a stop and was off the animal's back, looking every bit the cowboy in his jeans, Western shirt, boots and the Stetson on his head. Her husband was a gorgeous man, regardless of whether he was wearing navy attire or dressed as he was now. She could see him riding the range of the forty-acre ranch they now owned.

A ranch she had yet to tell him about.

He rushed over to her. "Why did you leave like that, Teri?"

She lifted her chin. "Honestly? What else was I to say, Mac?"

He reached out and pulled her into his arms. "I'm sorry, baby," he murmured brokenly. "I'm sorry you went through that alone. I'm sorry I wasn't there for you. And I would have wanted our baby, please know that."

She fought back tears when she lifted her head to look up at him. "I know that, Mac. I never doubted that you would. But what hurts more than anything is that I lost the son we wanted." And then she buried her face in his chest and sobbed.

Mac held his wife while she cried. The sound nearly broke his heart. He felt like an ass for saying what he had earlier without knowing all the facts. And now that he did know, he hurt right along with her.

He'd always wanted a big family and so had Teri. Using sound judgment, they'd decided to stop at four. It was hard enough for Teri to handle everything alone when he was gone on his missions, without adding another child to their family. But that hadn't meant they would not have welcomed a fifth. She was a wonderful mother to his kids. He knew that. He also knew that after having four girls they'd entertained the idea of trying again for a son but had decided not to. There was no guarantee their fifth child would be a boy.

But it had been.

He gently stroked her back, wondering what had caused the miscarriage. He was about to ask when she pushed herself out of his arms. "I need time alone, Mac. Please leave."

He shook his head. "There's no way I'm going back to the cabin and leave you out here."

"No, I don't want you to do that. I want you to leave and go back to Virginia. I'll be home in a few days and we'll talk some more then."

Mac knew he had to be looking at her like she'd lost her mind. "I'm not going anywhere and leaving you here, Teri. Whatever happens in our marriage we're in this together. We—"

"No, Mac. With you it's never really 'we.' Not really. It's what you want and what you think, and like the good wife, I fall in line. But you know what, Mac? I didn't know how much I wanted another baby until I found out I was pregnant. Then I wanted it with everything within me. I didn't care about how difficult it would be, or how you and I can't seem to agree, because I knew we would make it work."

"Teri—"

"No, you always want me to do what you want, Mac. You never ask what I want. Like how I want to work."

"That's not fair. You knew how I felt about things before we married. Is it wrong for a man to want to take care of what's his?" he asked, not liking the way their conversation was going.

"Only when you start taking our marriage for granted."

He didn't say anything for a minute and then he asked her, "And you honestly think I've done that?"

"All I know is that I woke up yesterday morning feeling sad and depressed, and a part of me wished you were here with me."

"I am here with you now, Teri. I want to spend the rest of the week here with you. We can consider it a second honeymoon. We can—"

"No, I don't need a second honeymoon, Mac. I need a marriage with a husband who won't question everything I do when he returns home. If you stay here, we will only argue...especially when I tell you about the other thing."

Mac lifted a brow. Did that mean there was more? "What other thing?"

She shook her head. "I don't want to talk about it now. I need time alone, Mac. Please go home and stay with the girls until I return. When I get back on Sunday, I'll tell you everything."

"I am not leaving."

At that moment the sound of the horses caught their attention. Both animals were fidgeting, acting anxious and prancing about as if they were trying to get away.

"I wonder what's wrong with them," she said.

"I don't know," he replied, and they moved toward the animals to find out for themselves.

Mac glanced around. Had they picked up the scent of a wolf, coyote or some other wild animal? The closer he and Teri got to the horses, the more agitated the animals seemed to get.

"Oh, my God, Mac. Look!"

The frantic sound of Teri's voice had him looking over at her. She was pointing toward the sky. He saw it. Damn.

In the distance was a gigantic tornado. It had already touched down and was swirling right in their direction.

Five

"We need to get the hell out of here!" Mac said, pulling Teri toward the horses.

"And go where? We're not going to be able to outrun that, Mac."

"I know. I recall passing several abandoned mineshafts coming here," he said, untying her horse and handing her the reins.

"But we'll be headed toward the twister," Teri said, climbing on Amsterdam's back.

"We have no choice. If we stay here, we'll be out in the open. Our chances would be better trying to get to a mine before that damn tornado does. That means we'll need to ride like hell to get there."

Teri had no problem doing that and knew Mac didn't, either. "Then let's go."

She took off and Mac kept up with her. They had to tighten their hold on the reins to control the horses. Animals had an instinct to avoid danger and they were forcing their steeds head-on toward it.

"It's okay, boy." She leaned in to whisper to Amsterdam. "It's okay."

As if the horse believed her, he picked up speed. And even through the sense of impending doom, Teri couldn't help smiling. From the moment Amsterdam had been selected as the horse for her during her stay, she believed they had bonded.

She glanced over at Mac and knew he had gone into SEAL mode, intent on keeping them alive, regardless of the danger. She doubted he'd talked to his horse, yet the animal seemed to accept the man on his back was master and wherever he led the horse had to go, regardless of whether he wanted to or not.

"We're almost there. I can see the windmill,"

Mac shouted over to her. She nodded against the wind that had picked up and she refused to look toward the sky. She just refused to do so.

They reached the area and quickly got off the horses. While Teri removed the saddlebags from the animals' backs, Mac grabbed a huge, thick limb off the ground and used it to knock some of the boards from one of the mineshaft openings. She released the horses, knowing their instinct for survival would have them running away to find refuge from the storm.

After the horses raced off, Teri rushed over to Mac. "Why did you decide on this particular mineshaft?" she asked him as she began helping to move the boards aside.

"The wider opening will afford more air to circulate. It also looks sturdier than the others and the ground around here is damp. That means there's water somewhere in this shaft."

Teri glanced down at the ground. She hadn't noticed that. At that moment she looked up to see several limbs from a huge tree blown down near their feet.

"Get in. I'll take the saddlebags."

"I'll help."

Mac looked at her, opened his mouth as if he was about to protest but then changed his mind, and said, "Come on. We need to hurry."

Teri had never been in a mineshaft before and glanced around. The area inside was dark. She could barely see in front of her. When suddenly a light appeared, she saw it was the flashlight from Mac's cell phone. It shone brighter than the one on hers.

"We need to get as far away from the opening as possible."

Heeding Mac's advice, she followed him deeper and deeper into the mineshaft, recalling horror stories of miners who got trapped underground and died for lack of air. "Let's place the saddles here," he said, placing his on the ground, and she followed, placing hers there.

They walked farther into the mineshaft when suddenly the ground beneath their feet began to shake. At the same time sediment began falling from the ceiling. Mac grabbed for her and she clutched him tight while he covered her body with his. Teri knew without being told that the twister was practically above them.

Although they were midway in the mineshaft, they could see debris flying around outside the mine's wide opening. They actually saw a tree, the same one she'd been standing under earlier, ripped from its roots to tumble down to the ground. Appliances, from no telling where, had gotten caught up in the twister and were tossed effortlessly to the ground.

Mac tried to press her face into his chest so she wouldn't see the devastation happening around them, but she looked anyway. Suddenly, the opening was covered in tree limbs, boards and other flying debris. She glanced up at Mac, and he didn't have to tell her they were trapped inside.

As if he sensed her thoughts, he leaned in close and said, "We'll be fine, Teri. Once it passes, we'll get out of here." She wanted to believe him. She *had* to believe him. They had four little ones at home who needed them.

Five minutes later, when everything went still, they knew the twister had moved on and everything was calm again. "I'm going to remove whatever is blocking the entrance so we can get out of here," Mac said.

"And I'll help you."

Mac and Teri worked together a good twenty minutes before finally accepting the inevitable. Unblocking the entrance wasn't going to be as easy as they'd hoped. In addition to the flying debris, there seemed to be something large blocking the entry. Teri had a feeling that huge windmill had collapsed.

"What do we do now?" she asked Mac. "Can you use your phone to call for help?"

Mac shook his head, obviously frustrated. "No, but the flashlight has at least eight hours of battery life. Let's use it to see if there's another way out of here."

Teri wondered if Mac actually thought there was, or if he was saying that to calm her fears. "Okay."

He didn't say anything more as they walked farther and farther into the mineshaft. Mac would pause every so often to study the walls around them, reaching out to touch a rocky surface or a wooded wall covered with thick dust. He looked around for a long moment before turning to her. "Not certain how sturdy some of these planks are we're walking on, so watch your step."

"I'll be careful, Mac."

As if he assumed she wouldn't, he took her hand in his. She started to pull it back but figured doing such a thing would be childish. He was only making sure she was okay and wasn't going to take any chances. A part of her couldn't help appreciating his protectiveness; she knew that was an ingrained part of Mac and who he was.

When she'd met him, he'd been a SEAL and she had married him knowing what that kind of life meant for her. It hadn't mattered. She had loved him. They'd been different as day and night in how they dealt with life in general but they had always managed to work through it. As their marriage had grown, so had they. But lately it seemed they were encountering more and more roadblocks. He seemed to have less faith in her ability to handle things without his input. Was this what it meant for couples to grow apart?

She glanced over at him and saw how he was

walking slowly and with purpose as he continued to take in their surroundings. There was a question she had to ask him. "Mac?"

He turned to her. "Yes?"

"Is our air supply limited in here?"

He held her gaze as if he was trying to decide how much to tell her. He then said, "Yes, somewhat, but not as much as I figured it would be."

"Why do you say that?"

"Because vegetation is covering some of the rocks."

She'd noticed it, too, but hadn't thought much about it. "And?"

"And in order for anything to grow in here it would need a sufficient amount of air, water and sunshine. I figure there is water coming from somewhere, probably some underground canal. But I'm not sure about the sunshine. This mineshaft shouldn't be anything more than a black hole in the earth's surface, and I haven't figured out the atmospheric piece yet."

She nodded. "I wonder how long it's been boarded up."

He shrugged massive shoulders that she had

to admit looked good in his Western shirt.
"There's no telling."

They continued walking and he held tight to
her hand. When was the last time they'd held
hands? Honestly, she shouldn't be wondering
about that now, but she couldn't help doing
so. When was the last time they'd taken time
to just spend together? Just the two of them,
away from the kids? Whenever he returned
home, he slept the first day off. After that he
had to readjust to the role of husband and father and would immediately want to become
king of the castle. When that happened, his
attitude would clash with hers.

Then there were always the numerous activities the kids were involved with, too many
for them to set aside "daddy and mommy"
time. All four girls were active in something.
Even Tasha had started taking piano lessons
at an early age. Several people had told them
they thought their youngest daughter would
grow up to be a gifted pianist one day. While
Mac was home it was important to him to be
there and share in their training, progress and
achievements. Their daily schedules were full

and to take off in search of time for each other seemed like a selfish act. Now more than ever she saw how such togetherness was needed for couples.

Dr. Blum had tried to encourage them during their counseling sessions to carve out periods for themselves. They'd said they would and it was then that Mac had promised to take her on a second honeymoon to Torchlight. But they had never found the opportunity and at some point had stopped making the effort to try. Now they were here, a couple still in the same predicament they'd been when they sought Dr. Blum's services.

"Well, what do we have here?"

Skirting around boards and makeshift walls, they came upon what had once been a storage room. Shelves were stocked with several kinds of canned goods. Teri moved closer to see tuna, peaches and dry milk. There were also several huge water barrels.

Mac checked out the barrels, smiled and gave a thumbs-up. "They are full, but I suspect there's an additional water channel somewhere in here, which is even better."

Teri nodded. "What type of place do you think this was?"

He glanced over at her. "I would guess it's what they thought of as their shelter—where food, water and supplies were kept. Usually, it's where they would bed down for the night when they weren't in the productive mines. I wouldn't be surprised if there are sleeping quarters somewhere in here."

Teri studied Mac. "You seem knowledgeable about mines."

He nodded. "Not as much mines as caves. Part of my duties as a SEAL is to scout and find the best place for us to hunker down whenever we're in hostile territory. A cave is where we were holed up most of the time while in Syria. Being out in the open in a camp is too risky."

He glanced around before saying, "SEALs have a knack of making caves appear inhabitable. You wouldn't believe how many times our enemies were right there, outside the entrance of the cave, and we were able to listen to their every word. Once we overheard them strategize their entire plan of attack against us."

Teri wondered if Mac realized this was the first time he'd ever talked about his work as a navy SEAL and the danger he faced. Whenever he returned home it was as if he needed to put out of his mind whatever mission he'd gone through. Like that time a couple of years ago, when he'd assumed his teammate Laramie "Coop" Cooper had gotten killed, and Mac had shut up his emotions. No matter how she'd tried, she hadn't been able to tear through the grieving wall he'd erected.

"Ready to move on?"

She looked up at him. "Ready whenever you are."

Teri didn't want to think about how differently things might have turned out if he'd left when she'd asked him to leave earlier. Or if he hadn't come after her at all. She would have tried to outrun the twister and would probably have died doing so. She had begun resenting Mac's presence, but now she appreciated it.

She tightened her hold on his hand and they moved forward, going deeper and deeper toward the back of the mine.

* * *

Teri had stopped asking questions and Mac thought that was a good thing. He hadn't given her a straight answer when she asked about how much air they had. In addition to his concern regarding lack of oxygen, he was worried about the possibility of poisonous gases in the air.

Knowing this particular mineshaft had been used as a shelter facility was a good thing. He couldn't tell for sure just how good until they checked out the place more. At least they had water and food for a while. But the uncertainty about the air component bothered him.

Nowadays most mineshafts were equipped with emergency kits that included portable devices providing a supply of breathable oxygen in case anyone got trapped underground, or should any type of poisonous gases leak into the air. Other kits contained small tanks filled with oxygen to which a miner had immediate access. He would love having either about now.

He figured this particular mine had undergone its share of digging and blasting, which accounted for the worn-looking internal structure. Typically mines, especially those used as shelters, had escape tunnels. If this one had such a thing, he was determined to find it.

He suddenly stopped when he heard a sound and immediately placed Teri behind him.

"Mac? What is it?" she asked, whispering close to his ear.

"I thought I heard something."

It wasn't uncommon for wild animals to take refuge in deserted mines. With that thought in mind, he eased his hunting knife from his pocket and immediately his stance went into an attack mode. He waited and when he didn't hear the sound again, he relaxed somewhat.

"False alarm."

"What do you think the sound was?" Teri asked him.

"Probably the shifting of the foundation. There's no telling what all has fallen in on top of us." He glanced up and wondered if there was a chance the ceiling might collapse down on them. It didn't look too solid.

Checking his watch, Mac saw it was late afternoon. Chances were the authorities were out trying to assess damage in the region. Because of the magnitude of that tornado he figured there had been extensive destruction over a wide area. He hoped everyone had time to take shelter and that there weren't any casualties. But he'd seen that tornado, had witnessed its power and knew a number of places were flattened to the ground by now.

Because the cabin Teri had reserved was so far from the main house, there was no telling how long it would take before they were missed. Would the authorities assume they were in the house and look for them there? If the horses returned without riders would that clue them in? He knew that wouldn't necessarily be the case since they'd removed the saddles from the horses' backs.

Mac knew that meant they had to assume no one would be looking for them. Not totally true. He knew a certain group would come looking for him eventually. Namely his SEAL teammates. They would know he was alive and wouldn't give up until they found him.

When he heard Teri's stomach growl he remembered how late it was and realized they'd missed a meal. They wouldn't be eating by candlelight but at least they would be sharing a meal together.

Tightening his hand on hers, he said, "Come on, let's go back to where those canned goods were and get something to eat."

Bane Westmoreland heard the beeping of his phone and recognized it for what it was. It was an alert from one of his teammates. He eased away from his wife's side, hoping not to wake her, but he wasn't surprised when her eyes flew open. He should have known that with three-year-old triplets she didn't know the meaning of sound sleep, especially since it was four in the afternoon. Early on they had learned to take a nap whenever the triplets took theirs.

"That's my SEAL phone," he said, leaning over to kiss her on the lips.

"Do you think they're calling you back for another assignment this soon? You haven't been home but two days," Crystal said, pulling up beside him in bed.

"No, that's not it. That ringtone is from one of the guys. I'll be back in a minute."

He left his bedroom to go into the kitchen, walking over several toys to do so. Glancing out the window, he could see the structure of his home that was still under construction in the distance. He and Crystal had met with the builders that day and had been told their home would be ready in a few months. They were looking forward to moving in. There would definitely be more room for their three-year-old triplets. His cousin Gemma, the interior designer in the family, would be coming all the way from Australia to decorate.

He sat down at the kitchen table and called Coop when he saw the alert had come from him. "What's up, man? I know you aren't calling again for tips on how to get your daughter to sleep." Coop and his wife, Bristol, had a four-year-old son named Laramie and a one-and-a-half-year-old daughter named Paris.

"No, that's not it. Teri and Mac are missing."

Bane sat up straight. "What do you mean they are missing?"

"I take it you haven't been watching the news."

Bane rubbed a hand down his face. "No. Crystal and I decided to grab a nap while the kids took theirs."

"Then you wouldn't know about that tornado that ripped through the outskirts of Cheyenne, namely the town of Torchlight, a little more than an hour ago. And it was a bad one. Already the death toll has reached double digits."

Bane released a whistle, as he stood to his feet. "Mac is still alive," he said with certainty.

"Yes, our tracker says he is, but they're listed as missing for now. Mac's parents called our commanding officer after they were notified Mac and Teri are among those unaccounted for. I'm letting the others know we need to head out for Wyoming."

Bane nodded. "I'll see you in Torchlight."

David Holloway, known by family and friends as Flipper, glanced around the table. He was with his family, dining at their favorite restaurant in Dallas as they celebrated his brother's announcement that he would be remarrying in a few months. The woman his brother was marrying was none other than a cousin of Swan, Flipper's wife. His brother Liam had met Jamila Fairchild at his and Swan's wedding a year and a half ago.

Everyone was happy for the couple, especially his parents, Colin and Lenora Holloway. He knew they'd been worried about Liam, especially after his split with Bonnie over five years ago. He hadn't dated anyone seriously since then. He'd concentrated on being the perfect dad to his little girl.

Flipper noted the size of the Holloway family was growing. Now it included his parents, their five sons and four of those sons' wives, their grandkids, and Jamila, soon to be the newest addition to the family. Flipper and his brothers were close to his parents. Their loving and tight-knit relationships had been the reason none of their sons had had any qualms about settling down and marrying. Unfortunately, the woman his brother Liam had married the first time around had been bad news. The only good thing that had come from the union was their little girl.

Something else others found unique about his family was that his father had retired as a SEAL commander-in-chief. All five of his sons had followed in his footsteps to become SEALs, as well.

After congratulations were said by all, his father made a toast to welcome Jamila to the family. Flipper could tell from the huge smile on Swan's face that she was happy for the cousin with whom she shared a very close relationship. Although he and Swan made their home in Key West, they visited the family in Dallas every chance they got.

His cell phone went off and he recognized the ringtone. Excusing himself from the table, he moved to a different area to take Coop's call. He returned a few minutes later with a grim look on his face.

"What's wrong, Flipper?" his father asked him.

When all eyes went to him, he said, "That was Coop. A tornado went through Wyoming a few hours ago, not far from Cheyenne. The media is saying it's one of the deadliest to hit the area. Coop got a call from our commander-in-chief. Mac and Teri were there and now they're missing."

"Missing?" It seemed everyone at the table asked all at once.

"Yes, he and Teri were on a dude ranch there. The entire ranch was destroyed, and Mac and Teri can't be found. So they're listed as missing."

He turned to Swan. "I'm leaving tonight to go help find Mac."

"I'm joining you. I can leave tomorrow," Liam said.

"Don't leave us out." His other three brothers agreed to join them.

Flipper wasn't surprised. Because Mac had been a part of his life since his first day as a SEAL—as a teammate, another older brother and a mentor—he had won a special place in the hearts of Flipper's family members.

"Great. We'll need all the help we can get."

"What do you mean Mac is missing?" Viper asked Coop, struggling to prop his cell phone on his shoulder close to his ear, while handing their two-year-old son to his wife, Layla.

His words, he noticed, had given her pause, as well.

He'd been out teaching his son, Gavin Blake IV, how to ride a pony. Gavin was at the same age Viper had been when he'd been taught to ride. He listened as Coop gave him the details about the tornado that had touched down near Wyoming, destroying the dude ranch where Mac and Teri had been staying.

"I'm calling everyone so we can get together and find Mac," Coop informed him.

"That's good. I'm leaving tonight."

"Okay. I'll see you then." Coop clicked off the phone knowing they never ceased being a team whether they were on duty or off. That was the SEAL way and for them, the only way.

Six

Mac used his knife to open the cans of tuna and thought the tin mugs from the saddlebags came in handy for water. They had turned over empty water barrels to sit on. Being the ever-efficient mom that she was, Teri never left home without a travel-size bottle of hand sanitizer and pulled it out of her saddlebag.

"This is all we have to eat for now. At least until I scope out the place to find what else might be here."

Teri glanced over at her husband. "No problem. Tuna and water are okay. Besides, I need to lose a few pounds."

"No, you don't. You look good. You always look good."

Teri smiled at her husband's compliment. He would tell her that often enough, but always when they were naked and about to make love. Never when she'd been fully dressed. "Thanks, but losing a few pounds won't hurt."

"If you say so."

She glanced over at him to see what changes she could notice since he'd left eight months ago. There were always invisible changes she wouldn't know about, so for now she would concentrate on the visible ones. He looked more built than ever. Even more alluring. She thought the same thing now that she'd thought when she'd first seen him that night at the rodeo: Thurston McRoy was a handsome man with rakish good looks.

Ten and a half years of marriage hadn't lessened her desire for him, not when he took such good care of himself. But then, he really didn't have a choice. Being a SEAL, especially a member of Team Six, the most highly trained elite forces in the US military, meant being physically fit at all times, and he was certainly that.

Facial hair used to annoy him, but because of the covert operations he'd been involved in lately, a beard had become the norm. However, as soon as he returned home, he would shave. Evidently, coming directly after her had robbed him of the time to do so.

"Is something wrong, Teri? You're staring at me."

She met his gaze. "No. I didn't mean to stare. Just trying to see any changes."

He shrugged. "Why do you expect there will be any?"

Now it was her time to shrug, although she could tell him of a few reasons. Like the time he'd gotten stabbed and hadn't told her until she'd seen the wound for herself. Or that time a bullet had grazed his ear. However, she wouldn't bring any of that up. "No reason."

Things got quiet between them as they ate and she was determined not to let him catch her staring again. But then she could feel him staring at her and she was tempted to glance over at him and ask why he was staring, just like he'd asked her.

It was hard, nearly impossible, not to remember all those sexual fantasies she had about him whenever he was gone. Fantasies he was usually accommodating to play out when he returned and she told him about them. So why was she not telling him about those fantasies now when she'd definitely had a few? Actually, there had been more than a few.

"What happened, Teri? How did you lose the baby? Please tell me what happened."

His words intruded into her thoughts. A part of her didn't want to talk about it, especially not now. But then, she knew he deserved to know and that now was probably the best time to tell him. They had this time alone, where neither of them could walk out. They needed to use it to talk, and she meant really talk about issues that concerned them and their marriage.

Teri wasn't sure what to say. She could tell him just what the doctor said, or she could talk about what she suspected, which the doctor claimed was just guilt and not fact. She had not been restricted from flying. And she'd given birth to four kids with no problem. The only difference between those pregnancies and her recent fifth was that she'd gotten on a plane to travel somewhere during her first four months.

She glanced over at Mac. "The doctor said it was just one of those things, that up to one in five pregnancies end in miscarriage before twenty weeks."

"And you didn't do anything different?"

Was that accusation she heard in his voice? She didn't want to believe that it was and knew she was allowing her feelings of guilt to make her defensive. "I hadn't done anything that Dr. Gleason felt would have had a bearing on the pregnancy. I told him everything I'd been doing, and according to him none of it mattered. Like I told you, he said it was just one of those things and nothing I did contributed to it."

What she'd told him was the truth. He didn't have to know about the inner turmoil within her.

"Did you see the girls while you were home?" she asked, hoping to change the subject.

* * *

Mac knew his wife well enough to know when she wasn't being totally forthcoming about something. What was it that she wasn't telling him? And why? He intended to find out in due time. He wouldn't press her about it now.

"Yes, I saw the girls. Everyone was asleep except for Tasha. I think her eyes opened the moment I walked into the room. It was as if she knew I was home."

Teri chuckled. "Figures. I think she has a built-in radar where you're concerned."

"Just like her mama has a built-in radar whenever I'm home?"

Teri didn't say anything because that much was true. Whenever Mac was home it was as if her senses needed to know where he was every second. She tried not to worry about him while he was away on an assignment, instead depending on Bane, Viper, Coop and Flipper, the four SEAL teammates he was close to, to keep him safe. She wouldn't even discount Nick Stover. Although Nick was no longer a SEAL and now worked for Homeland

Security, Mac still spoke of him often and included him in the mix even now.

As far as she was concerned, those five looked up to Mac and considered him an older brother since Mac had been a SEAL a few years before them. To hear Mac tell it, he looked out for them, but she was sure it worked the other way around, as well. She was counting on it because she knew her husband could be a hothead at times, although he claimed he wasn't. But still, as much as she tried not to worry, as much as she assured herself she really didn't have to, she always did anyway.

"Yes, just like her mama has her radar," she finally said.

"So, tell me about your radar, Teri McRoy. Why are you so tuned in to me whenever I'm home?"

Teri thought that in all the years of their marriage, he'd never asked her to explain her actions whenever it came to him. Now she could speak freely and share her inner feelings about this particular topic. "I worry about you when you're home, Mac."

She knew it was silly because if anyone

could take care of themselves, it was Mac. But because of her deep, unyielding need to pro-tect him, she was very much tuned in to him. She could sense his movements. She knew it used to drive him crazy but now he'd gotten accustomed to it.

"You don't have to worry about me, Teri."

"Easier said than done. I worry about you not getting enough rest before you have to be gone again. As your wife I want to make your life better, less stressful when you come home, but it seems all I do is make it more taxing. You always concentrate on what you think I've done wrong while you were gone and not any-thing I might have done right."

Did he?

Mac didn't say anything as he thought about what she had said. Were her feelings of being taken for granted justified? He rubbed his hands down his face. When was the last time he'd told her how proud he was of the way she was raising their kids? Or how he appreciated how she made their house into the home he looked forward to returning to? Or better yet, how much he loved her?

Instead, he would come home and start finding fault in the changes or additions she'd made without his input, knowing there were some decisions she had no choice but to make without him.

He looked over at her. "I see what you've done right every time I return home and walk into the house, Teri. The girls are beautiful, well behaved, respectful and doing great in school. My home is my castle and you make it so. I teased you about your radar but I love your attentiveness to me."

Mac paused a moment and then added, "Even with all we have, I worry a lot about our finances. It's something I can't help doing."

She lifted her chin. "I can understand that due to your background, but do you have to be so critical? So obsessive about my decisions, Mac? Do Bane, Viper, Coop and Flipper question every single penny their wives spend?"

In a way her question irritated him because she knew the answer. "No, but then, they don't have to. Bane and Coop were born to wealth and Viper's and Flipper's families aren't exactly poor, Teri. My parents were still paying for student loans when me and my sister were born. There was no money for my parents to inherit or to pass on to their offspring. They worked hard, provided for me and my sister, but there was never any extra money to invest in generational wealth. I'm not complaining, and I don't resent my friends, trust me. They've helped me make more out of the little I started with. I have no problem making my own way."

As a SEAL he got bonuses, and for years he'd used a portion of those bonuses toward investments that were paying off. His daughters' college funds looked pretty damn good and he was proud of that. In truth, they had more than they needed. But he couldn't escape the feeling that it was never enough to feel secure. Though now he was feeling comfortable about getting that new house they wanted. He'd intended for that to be his surprise to her on his trip back home this time around.

"Trust me, I know, Mac." Then, as if she was ready to change the conversation to something else, she asked, "Are we ever going to get out of here? For all anyone knows we're at that cabin and may not have been missed."

He could hear the worry in her voice. "When they find out we aren't there, they'll come looking for us."

"Yes, but will they know to look for us here?"

If she meant the authorities, then no, they wouldn't know. But he knew of four men, with the help of a fifth, who would. And he felt certain they would find them. He could arrest her fears about them being found but then he would have to explain why he was so certain of it, and he couldn't do that. It was a pact the six of them had made after that time when they'd thought they had lost Coop, whose captors led everyone to believe they had killed him. Instead he'd been held as prisoner in the Syrian mountains for nearly a year. That had been the hardest year of their lives, believing Coop was dead. When they'd gotten word he was alive, their SEAL team had gone in and rescued him. Their enemies had tried breaking his body but they couldn't break his spirit.

Coop had said that what had kept him going was his belief that his teammates would eventually come and rescue him. And they had.

After that, Mac and his teammates had decided they never wanted to experience again what they'd gone through with Coop. So, when Nick had told them of this microchip tracking device that was more technologically advanced than any on the consumer market, they'd signed up to be the first to try it. The microchip was inserted under the skin of their right hands and no one knew of the implant other than their commanding officer, who had to approve the procedure. With the microchip, if any of the six of them went missing, they could be tracked to their precise location by latitude, longitude and altitude. Not only that, their body movement could be detected and studied to determine pain level due to the possibilities of injuries. The chip could also sense any other life-threatening symptoms emitted through brain waves. He knew his teammates would be testing the tracker's abilities for the first time with him.

He and Teri were fine for now with enough

food and water to last a couple of days. His biggest concern was oxygen—how long would they be able to breathe, shut up underground like this? He wouldn't talk to Teri about it for fear she would worry.

"Mac, will they know to look here?"

His thoughts were pulled back to Teri when she repeated what she'd asked him earlier. A question he hadn't answered. "Not sure, but it doesn't matter."

She frowned. "Why doesn't it matter?"

"Because once Bane, Coop and the others get wind that I'm missing, they'll come looking for us."

She nodded. "You're certain of that?"

"Yes."

"But will they be able to find us, or will they assume we're somewhere in the vicinity of the cabin?"

He smiled over at her. "They are SEALs, Teri. They will figure things out."

"But will they do it in time?"

"They will find us in time."

He saw uncertainty in her eyes. Reaching out, he slid her hand into his and entwined their fingers. "Trust me, baby. I won't let anything happen to you."

She lifted her chin. "And I won't let anything happen to you, either."

He wanted to laugh at that, knowing he could do a better job of protecting her than she could of him. However, if thinking that way made her feel better and worry less he would give her that moment.

Smiling over at her, he said, "Okay, that's a deal. We won't let anything happen to each other. Now let's get rid of this trash and then figure out how and where we need to bunker down for the night."

"Mac's alive and his brain waves aren't showing any signs of distress," Nick said, reading Mac's tracking data off his computer. The tracking devices the six of them wore were manned by Nick since he was the most computer savvy of the group. Any of the others could step in to be Nick's backup if it came to that, but Nick knew they were all hoping it never did.

"That's good to hear. I talked to Bane, Flipper and Viper earlier. We're all heading to Wyoming," Coop said.

"And I'm joining all of you. I'll be able to pinpoint his exact location once I get to the area and study maps of the surroundings."

"How soon do you think you'll get there?" Coop asked.

"Sometime tomorrow. I'll let Natalie know I'll be leaving and that she'll be on her own with the triplets for a while. In the meantime, I'll get periodic readings on Mac to relay to everyone."

"Thanks, Nick, and we'll see you in Wyoming."

Mac had taken her hand again and Teri didn't mind.

He did seem more capable of handling this sort of thing than she, but that didn't mean she wouldn't protect him if it came to that. She'd meant what she'd said about not letting anything happen to him, just like she knew he had meant what he'd said regarding protecting her.

"What if we don't find anything, Mac?"

He looked down at her. "There are blankets in the saddlebags."

She lifted a brow. "How do you know?"

"I checked."

When had he done that? "If we have blankets, then what are we looking for?"

"Something that could possibly serve as a cushion on the floor."

"Oh." He stopped walking and she glanced around. "This place is kind of messy, isn't it?"

He chuckled. "It's a mineshaft, Teri. Not a luxury condo."

"I know that but still you would think it could look better. A lot neater."

Mac checked the time on his watch. She'd noticed him doing that a lot. "What time is it now?" she asked him.

"Eighteen o eight."

She knew that meant 6:08 p.m. You couldn't be married to a military man without adjusting to their time, as well. Even the girls knew to convert to military time whenever he came home. It was dinnertime for most folks. She had a feeling dinner wouldn't be the same for a lot of people tonight.

"I was hoping to come across something like this sooner or later."

They had stumbled upon several horse troughs filled with hay. She was a cowgirl at heart so she understood the excitement that she heard in his voice. "Now I don't have to worry about sleeping on the hard ground tonight."

He glanced over at her. The intensity in his gaze nearly made her knees buckle. "There was never a time you would have had to sleep on the ground tonight or any night."

She lifted a brow. "So where would I have slept?"

He gave her that crooked smile she'd always thought was irresistible when he said, "I would have taken the floor and you would have slept on top of me. Granted we would have gotten little sleep."

The serious look on his face made her heart pound because she believed what he said to be true. If their bodies touched in that way, fire would consume them and they would end up making love all over the place. Finding this hay was a good thing because the thought of sleeping on top of him gave her body sensuous shivers. Had she been tempted to sleep on him, she would be pregnant by the time they woke up tomorrow.

In the back of her mind, and slowly coming to the front, were memories of past lovemaking sessions with him. They would start off mating like rabbits because of the length of time they'd been apart. Then, after getting an hour or two of exhausted sleep, they would start another bout of lovemaking, proving how obsessed they were with each other and just how much they had missed each other.

It was during that second, slower time that they would try the positions their creative minds came up with. Just thinking of a few of those positions now actually brought color to her cheeks.

Mac thought it was rather cute that he could make his wife blush after ten years and four kids. No…five kids, he thought, feeling the loss of the one he hadn't known. His son. She had carried him inside her for four months, which meant she had gotten to spend time with him, develop a bond. Mac regretted he hadn't even been there to give her a tummy rub or to place his ear to her belly to hear his child moving inside her.

He had missed out on all those things.

"Well, now that won't be necessary."

He glanced back over at her and forced a wry smile to his lips. "You can still lie on top of me, though."

She met his gaze. "Like I said, that won't be necessary."

"Maybe not necessary but better."

Although the flashlight from his cell phone was holding its own, there wasn't a lot of light. But it was enough to see her. He thought now what he'd thought the first time he'd seen Teri. His wife was a stunner.

Not only that, she was a pretty damn intelligent woman to boot. And he couldn't forget what a great body she had. Slim waist, luscious hips, mouthwatering breasts and one hell of an ass. Whether she knew it or not, thoughts of her kept him going. Made him appreciate being a man.

A man who always returned home to her.

Then why did they argue so much when he got there?

He remembered what that marriage counselor had told him. He was a man who seemed programmed to sweat the small stuff. He knew that was true. He'd tried to change and for a little while he had. Just until his next assignment. When he'd returned home, he'd slowly slipped back into his old ways.

"Better for what, Mac?"

It was hard to stay focused around her. "Better when we make love again." He couldn't think of any better way to pass the time. He glanced over at all that hay. It would certainly serve a good purpose.

"We won't be making love again."

His head snapped around to look at her. "Excuse me?"

She drew in a deep breath and those luscious breasts moved in a tantalizing way when she did so. "I said we won't be making love again. We can't."

Hmm, maybe he needed to refresh her memory.

"We did. Yesterday. Last night. Before daylight this morning."

She nervously nibbled on her bottom lip. That delicious bottom lip. Intrigued, he studied her. He hadn't seen her do that in a while. She was uptight about something. What?

"I know but we can't do it again."

He lifted a brow. "Why? Last time I looked we were married, which means we can do just about anything, Teri."

"But we shouldn't have."

He heard the agitation in her brusque tone. What the hell was going on here? An awkward silence ensued between them as he looked at her. He was tempted to check her forehead for a possible fever. He'd never, ever recalled a time when they had to put the brakes on making love. They both enjoyed it.

"There must be a reason you think that, Teri," he said in what he hoped was his calmest voice. "You want to explain it to me?"

She didn't say anything for a minute. "There are two reasons, Mac. First, making love only serves as a Band-Aid on a festering wound between us. It's time to stop resorting to temporary solutions and try to heal the wound."

She made it sound like what was going on between them was something they couldn't work out. She had committed herself to his way of life when they married. It had been her choice to agree to move around the world whenever he got a new assignment, her choice to forgo her career to advance his. She'd always seemed understanding of those times he hadn't been there for special occasions and holidays and had done a great job of holding it together for him and their family.

"We'll get through this, Teri."

"How? By making love? I'm tired of you thinking that's all it will take. What about my feelings, Mac? I need more from you than sex. I need for you to understand my feelings, trust my decisions, respect my role not only when you're gone but also when you return home. I need to feel appreciated and like I'm not being taken for granted."

He took in everything she'd said. "Okay, now what's the other reason?"

She nibbled on her bottom lip again before

saying, "The reason is something I should have told you yesterday…before we made love."

"Then tell me now," he said, trying to keep the frustration out of his voice.

"It's me."

His gaze roamed all over her, and in his mind, she was still the sexiest woman on a pair of gorgeous legs. "What about you?"

She began nibbling on those lips once again. "Teri," he said in an impatient voice. "What about you?"

She met his gaze and held it. "I'm not on any type of birth control."

Seven

Teri watched Mac go still, as if he'd been frozen in place. He was probably standing there remembering how many orgasms they'd shared within the last twenty-four hours. Enough to make a lot of babies if science worked that way. It didn't. But it had been more than enough times to make one.

"Any reason you didn't tell me before now?"

She could give him plenty of reasons, but they would all come back to one. The main one. "I had missed you and at the time I desperately needed to connect with you."

"Okay, I can understand that."

She knew he could understand because that was the reason they would make love often whenever he came home. Time apart always made them miss each other and want each other more. They couldn't wait to connect intimately. But then when their mating frenzies were over, they would be at odds with each other over one thing or another...like they were now.

"So why didn't you restart the pill after your pregnancy? You knew I was coming home sooner or later."

Whether he realized it or not, he was questioning her actions. Again. It bothered her whenever he did that. "I had rescheduled the surgery and figured I would have it done before you returned."

"You rescheduled the surgery?"

"Yes, it's scheduled for next week. That's one of the reasons I came here. I needed to come to terms with losing the baby and to stay focused on what we'd agreed to do and what it would mean to me."

He didn't say anything for the longest time and then he said, "Did it ever occur to you after losing the baby that proceeding with the surgery was something we needed to talk about?"

She raised an eyebrow. "No, that never occurred to me, Mac. The decision had already been made by us, and I honestly didn't think it would be back up for discussion, regardless of my pregnancy. I know how you can act when I go back on any decisions we've made together."

He stared at her for a long moment without saying anything. Then he turned and grabbed a huge armful of hay before walking off.

I know how you can act when I go back on any decisions we've made together.

Teri's words hit him hard in the gut. As he made several trips back to the trough for hay, he couldn't say anything but he did dwell on what she'd said. She had done a good job of reminding him just what an ass he could be at times. An inflexible ass.

Why was it so hard for him to loosen his grip on control? Mainly because he didn't see it as control but as looking out for someone. In this case, Teri and the girls.

He'd never intended for Teri to work outside the home once they started having kids. She'd known it and had seemed fine with the thought of being a stay-at-home mom. She'd loved children as much as he did, and they wanted a houseful. Only, things were hard with a household. He didn't want to add to Teri's burden while he was away, and they'd decided to call it quits at three. Then they'd agreed for a fourth, hoping it would be a boy, but regardless, a fourth child was the limit. They had enough love and money for four, but part of him couldn't help remembering how he'd grown up. The hardship. Mentally, the cost felt high, especially with all the activities in their children's futures and the rising cost of college educations.

The decision not to have any more kids had been one they'd both been okay with. For him her unexpected pregnancy was a game changer. Maybe it should not have been, but it was. At least for him, and he felt bad that she couldn't see that.

What if he'd come home two weeks from now instead of two days ago? She would have had the surgery by then. And what bothered him more than anything was that she felt that was what he would have expected. He wished he could claim that she didn't know him at all, if she believed that, but all he could say was that she thought it because she *did* know him.

When Mac returned with the last load of hay, he glanced over at Teri and saw what she'd done. She had separated the hay into two stacks to make separate beds for them. That was quite obvious now that she'd spread the blankets over the hay. Did she honestly think they wouldn't be sleeping together?

"What are you doing, Teri?"

Without looking up she said, loud enough for him to hear, "What does it look like I'm doing?"

Mac rubbed a hand down his face in frustration. "We aren't going to have separate beds. It's going to get cold tonight."

She looked up at him. "It won't be the first time I've had to keep myself warm, Mac."

That was a low blow, he thought. Was she

itching for a fight? If so, one quick way to do it was to start complaining about the time he was gone from home as a SEAL. She'd known the score when she married him.

"Fine. Suit yourself."

She would discover soon enough just how cold it got in here at night. It didn't matter one iota what season it was—autumn, winter, spring or summer—since they were practically buried beneath the earth.

"I'm turning out the light now," he said, just seconds before he did it.

"Why did you do that?" she asked and he could hear the near hysteria in her voice.

"To save the battery," he said. He figured the answer was obvious.

"I haven't gotten ready for bed."

What was there to get ready for? It wasn't as if they were at some hotel. They would be sleeping in their clothes. Tomorrow, when he hoped there would be more light, he would move around and explore. If there was another opening out of this place, he intended to find it.

He had dropped down to the bed of hay and

covered up with the blanket. He could hear movement where Teri was and wondered what she was doing but decided not to ask. He was following the advice of the marriage counselor they had gone to that time. He'd said, *When you feel yourself getting angry, allow yourself time to calm down and reflect and remember. Definitely remember. You have to force your mind to recall what drew the two of you together in the first place.*

His answer to that question was simple. It had been Teri's smile. It didn't just touch her lips but extended to her eyes, as well. Then it had been her body. It was definitely a body any man would love looking at. Then it had been her warm sense of humor.

It suddenly occurred to him that he saw less and less of that sense of humor each time he returned home. Why? Was any of that his fault? Probably. Just like it was his fault that she believed she had to have that surgical procedure done despite her unexpected pregnancy. He shifted in bed, thinking it was a damn shame he and Teri were doing something tonight they'd never done in the years they'd been married, which was to sleep in separate beds while he was home.

He figured she had a lot to think about and so did he. Tomorrow they would talk. When he heard the even sound of her breathing, he knew she'd drifted off to sleep and he allowed his eyes to drift closed to do the same. And he dreamed about how he'd made love to her that morning before she'd left to go riding.

How he'd kissed her awake with a desperation he wasn't aware he could experience. And how she had reciprocated, letting her tongue duel with his. He'd pulled her closer to him, not only needing to taste her but needing to feel her all over. His hands ran all over her naked body, down her back, before cupping her backside. He'd always loved the feel of her in his arms and this morning hadn't been an exception. He'd been gone for long periods of time before, but this had been one of the longest in years. He hadn't realized just how much he'd missed her until he'd begun making love to her.

And when he'd straddled her, the moan she'd

emitted when his hard erection had slid inside of her, pressing her into the mattress, spurred him to go deeper. The moment he was buried inside her he went still, savoring the feel of his engorged flesh held tight in her warm, wet body.

It took everything he had within, his total control as a SEAL, every ounce of restraint he possessed, not to explode inside of her at that moment. He'd fought the urge to do so. It had been the questioning look in her eyes, and then her question of, "What are you waiting for?" that had made him start moving. Made him thrust hard and then harder. It was that question that had made him tip his head back and growl while appreciating how it felt to sink deeper still into her body.

More than once he had to make sure she was right there with him, especially those times when he was a mere heartbeat away from climaxing. The room had been filled with her moans as he continued to stroke nonstop inside of her. Those moans of pleasure had driven him to kiss her harder and longer, and to thrust repeatedly inside her body.

As he drifted deeper and deeper into sleep in the recesses of his dreams, he could still hear those moans.

Teri woke up. No matter how much she tried, she couldn't get warm. She shifted her position again and had a feeling her toes were frozen. She needed Mac's body heat. Point-blank, she needed Mac. Besides, she owed him an apology.

She should not have made that wisecrack about being used to keeping herself warm. That hadn't been fair to him. She'd known what he did for a living when she married him but she couldn't imagine living without him. He couldn't keep her warm when he was gone and that wasn't his fault. And whenever he was home, he not only kept her warm on cold nights, but he also made her feel loved and protected. So why was he over there and she over here?

Because they'd had one of their disagreements, the ones that were happening way too often. But this time it was serious—it had included another life, one they'd shared in making. And she knew that, like always, any decisions on how they moved forward would be shared by them, as well.

Not able to stop shivering, she stood and grabbed her cover and moved over to where Mac lay. As if he'd been expecting her, Mac pulled himself up in a sitting position and reached out a hand to her. She grasped it and he drew her close to ease down beside him. He didn't say anything. Not even "I told you so." But then, that was Mac's way whenever he was proven right. He wouldn't dig it in. He probably figured swallowing her pride was enough humiliation.

When he practically wrapped his body into hers, she immediately felt warm and couldn't help sighing. "Thanks, Mac."

"Don't ever thank me for taking care of what's mine, Teri," he whispered close to her ear, causing her body to shiver again. However, this time it was for a different reason.

Teri knew that to anyone else, his words would sound too possessive, as if she was an object he owned. She knew that wasn't the case. He was merely stating what was the truth. She was his—heart, body and soul—like he was hers. But still, that made her wonder how two people so into each other the way they were could be at odds with each other as much as they were.

They had different personalities. She got that. The marriage counselor they'd met with for an entire three months had made sure they understood that. They'd been backsliding and now it was up to the both of them to get back on track. But the issues they were dealing with now were pretty major and he didn't know the half of it.

"Mac?"

"Yes."

"I'm sorry about what I said about you not being home to keep me warm on cold nights. I didn't mean it the way it sounded."

"No harm done."

She had found a comfortable position and was about to drift off when Mac's voice stopped her. "Teri?"

He shifted his body around to face her and automatically, she threw her leg over his thigh.

Too late she realized that wasn't a good move. "Yes?"

"I'm sorry you thought I would not have understood or supported your decision to delay having the surgery. I would have."

She didn't say anything for a minute. "Dr. Gleason told me I could reschedule the surgery a month ago but emotionally, I couldn't do it. I just wasn't ready. That's why it's scheduled for next week. At least it *was*."

There was no reason to tell him that it wouldn't be happening for a couple of reasons. First of all, even if they were rescued, there was no way she would feel up to having any type of surgery done. But the most important reason was that when they'd made love they hadn't used protection. That meant there was a possibility she could be pregnant now. Why didn't the thought of that bother her? In fact, the thought of having another baby lifted her spirits.

"And now you could be pregnant again."

His words had her looking over at him. So that possibility did occur to him. "Yes. How do you feel about that, Mac?"

"How would any man feel when the woman he loves carries his child? I just worry about your burden while I'm away. And I don't want our children to want for anything."

"You have always provided for us. The girls and I have never wanted for anything."

"But I want to give you more."

She wondered if he would ever realize that "more" wasn't everything and having each other was enough. "You can only do so much, Mac."

"How do you feel about us having another child, Teri?"

"Do you want me to be truthful?"

"No, Teri. I *expect* you to be truthful."

Yes, he would. "Then my answer is that I love the idea, Mac. Tasha is getting more independent and she doesn't want to be thought of as a baby anymore. She wants to be a big girl like Tatum and Tempest. I hate seeing my babies grow up."

"But they do," he said, being the voice of reason as usual.

"Yes, they do, and I know I can't replace one baby with another when that happens, Mac."

He didn't say anything for a minute. "I just worry about you, when I'm away. And I still think about how hard I had it growing up. I know that although we agreed not to have any more kids, deep down you would have been happy having a houseful."

He was right about that. She would love to have a houseful. Being the only child had been the pits.

"Yes, but I understood, Mac."

She loved her husband and knew carefully watching their finances was something he felt responsible for doing because of his background. Even though they had plenty. That made telling him about her purchase of the ranch that much harder.

"You said you have something else to tell me. What is it?"

Since they were talking, this would be the perfect opportunity to come clean and tell him everything. But she couldn't. It was lousy timing and she wasn't ready. However, she would be ready in the morning. She promised herself.

"Let's talk tomorrow, okay? I'm feeling sleepy, Mac."

He was quiet for a long moment and then he said, "All right, we'll talk tomorrow. Go to sleep."

Teri closed her eyes, appreciating her husband's body keeping her warm.

Eight

Mac woke up the next morning and immediately noticed two things. First and foremost, his wife was sleeping soundly in his arms and her too-tempting body was pressed close to him. Second, the level of oxygen in the air had changed. He didn't need a barometer to detect that. The pressure wasn't at an alarming level; it was even one he'd expected, but he was fully aware of the change. In fact, he had even predicted the level to be lower than what it was. That meant air was seeping into the mine from somewhere, and he was determined to find where.

He figured his teammates had heard he was missing about now and would be looking for them. He believed that. He had to believe that.

He glanced down at Teri. Why did he have a feeling there was something she wasn't telling him, something she was stalling? He wouldn't bring it up again but would let her decide when the best time would be. Hopefully, they would talk this morning as she'd said they would do. But now, while she slept, he would explore the mine without her. When he'd walked yesterday to where all that straw had been, he had felt moisture in the air. Today he would investigate where it was coming from.

Untangling their limbs, he eased from Teri's side, immediately missing the feel of her body. But separating himself from her was a good idea, especially since he'd maintained an erection all night. It wouldn't have taken much for him to break down and try coaxing her into making love with him. They'd taken a few chances already and she could very well be carrying his child.

Stretching the kinks out of his body he glanced back down at Teri again before moving away to explore the mine without her. It didn't take long for him to come to the area where they'd found all that hay. He kept moving. The deeper he went into the mineshaft, the more the air changed, and he could feel moisture, to the degree that the rock walls around him were damp in some places.

He smiled when he came across the small pool of crystal clear water. Nature never ceased to amaze him. He figured the water was a spill-off from that lake a few miles back. From the steam it generated he knew it was connected to some kind of underground heated spring.

He couldn't wait to bring Teri here. With that thought in mind, he headed back.

Laramie Cooper observed from beneath hooded lashes the man, a first responder, who was talking to Bane, Viper and Flipper. Coop had decided to hang back and check out their surroundings. He was certain that before the tornado had hit, this had been a pretty nice area. It reminded him of his spread in Texas. Now all he saw was devastation for miles. The majority of the trees were down and those left standing were barely doing so.

He suddenly turned his full concentration to the man because he'd offered his condolences, saying there was a chance Mac and Teri had not survived. The cabin where they'd been staying, as well as many others in the vicinity, had been flattened. A number of bodies had already been recovered, but not the McRoys'.

"And you won't recover them," Coop decided to say. "Thurston McRoy isn't dead."

The first responder, with an overly tired look, was about to reply to what Coop said when an approaching voice stopped the man. "I'll take over here, Floyd."

The man glanced over his shoulder, and then nodded. "Okay, Sheriff." He then walked off, his exhaustion apparent. The newcomer, who looked a little older but just as tired, faced them now and Coop quickly assessed him and concluded he was ex-military. It was his stance even under extreme fatigue. Before the man began speaking, Coop asked, "What branch of the military?"

The man turned his gaze to Coop, who'd moved to stand beside Bane, Viper and Flipper. As if he'd sized them up, he said, "I'm Sheriff Derwin Corilla, former marine." He then asked, "And you guys?"

It was Flipper who answered. "SEALs."

The man nodded, smiling. "I should have figured as much."

No one asked why. There had always been this rivalry between the navy and the marines but when it came to a mission and they were called to work together, they did. Most military men respected anyone who was willing to serve their country, no matter the branch.

Introductions were made, and Viper spoke up. "We share Coop's sentiments, Sheriff Corilla. Mac isn't dead."

Coop expected the man to ask why they were so certain. Instead he said, "I'm not going to go so far and say he isn't dead, but I don't think he or his wife were in that cabin when it came down."

"And why do you think that?" Bane asked.

Sheriff Corilla shifted his gaze to Bane. "Because we used the dogs and they didn't sniff out any bodies at the cabin. Then yesterday the two horses assigned to them to ride while they were here were found wandering the range, after having found refuge somewhere during the storm."

"They were saddled?" Viper asked.

"No, but one of my men, who is a trained horseman, checked them over and it looked as if they'd been ridden. I believe the McRoys had been out riding somewhere when the tornado hit. They must've set the horses free and hopefully found cover somewhere."

He paused and then said, "That tornado hit a vast area and we're still looking for survivors. I'm not giving up on anyone."

Coop nodded. "Not enough manpower." It was a statement and not a question.

Sheriff Corilla shook his head. "Is there ever? Right now, we're forming a search party to look for a seven-year-old kid who survived but somehow got away from his parents. So far we haven't found him."

"We're here to find Mac, but we'll be glad to help your guys out any way we can."

The man lifted a brow. "All four of you?"

Flipper grinned. "For now. To help find Mac we've called in the cavalry. A former team-mate who now works for Homeland Security is on his way here, and then my four brothers who are SEALs are coming, as well. Mac's kind of special to all of us."

"Even when we have to do our best to toler-ate him," Viper added, grinning, as well.

"We'll be glad to help look for that kid," Bane offered.

Corilla looked at Bane oddly, but he didn't question what he said, evidently accepting the SEALs had the rescue of the McRoys well under control. "In that case, thanks for the offer and I'll take any extra help we can get."

Viper nodded. "Then you got it."

Sheriff Corilla walked off.

Coop, Bane, Viper and Flipper glanced at each other. From their last phone conversa-tion with Mac, they concluded that as usual, he was in need of an attitude adjustment when it came to Teri. Maybe with them stranded to-gether they could use that time to hash out a few issues plaguing their marriage.

Nick had been monitoring Mac's brain waves

via the tracker and at present, there was no reason to think he was in immediate danger. When Nick arrived later that day, he would be able to pinpoint Mac and Teri's exact location.

In the meantime, they would join that search party.

Teri woke up to the sounds of Mac and glanced around to focus directly on him. The flashlight from his cell phone illuminated the area. He was shirtless, down to his briefs and exercising. Running in place. As she watched him her blood began running in place, as well, rushing like crazy through her veins.

Although the air was cool, he'd worked himself into a hefty amount of sweat. It covered his chest and drenched his hair. She had a workout routine, as well, but her regimen was definitely not as intense as his. She would join him sometimes when he was home and knew to stick to her own pace and not try to keep up with him. That attempt would be impossible.

As she lay there, she recalled she had slept in his arms and they hadn't made love. That was a miracle in itself since she and Mac were two people with high sexual energy. But that meant he'd accepted what she'd told him. Not only did they have issues to resolve, there was a chance those issues were now compounded by a possible pregnancy.

Mac finished his sets of running in place and bent over to draw in deep breaths. She loved watching him do that, as well. She pulled herself up. "Good morning, Mac."

He glanced over at her and when he did so, those dark, piercing eyes captivated her. As usual. "Good morning, Mrs. McRoy."

Teri smiled at him. She loved it when he called her that. It was a reminder that he'd chosen her, had given her that name to wear proudly and that made her his to claim. And she liked whenever he claimed her.

"Isn't exercising wasting air that we need?"

"Air has the ability to get in and out of places where people can't. I've noticed a fluctuation in oxygen levels in here, but never anything to be concerned about. It appears higher now than when I woke this morning, so I decided to take advantage of it and work out."

"I would join you, but I don't want to get all sweaty."

He chuckled. "A little sweat never hurt anyone."

"In my case it wouldn't be a little sweat. Whenever I work out with you, I tend to sweat a lot."

He chuckled. "That's what you get for trying to keep up with me."

"Trust me, Mac. I don't try keeping up with you. I'd be crazy to try, believe me. I work at my own pace."

He gave her an admiring nod and a sensuous smile that caught her low in her stomach. "In that case, you do a pretty good job of holding your own."

"I try."

"Then come try with me. You'll be glad to know you don't have to worry about the sweat. I'll wash it off you."

She lifted a brow. "Do we have that much water to waste?"

"Yes. I found a pool of clear water on the west end of this mineshaft."

Excitement filled her. "You did?"

The corners of his mouth lifted in another smile. "I did. Come join me."

She hesitated for a minute, remembering other times they'd exercised together and how they would shower together afterward. That always led to other things. Things they were better off not doing. He knew that, yet he was inviting her to work out with him anyway, with the promise of a shower afterward. He evidently had more willpower than she did. But then, she knew he honestly did.

"Okay. My muscles are kind of sore after a few days of riding Amsterdam."

He crossed the floor and offered her his hand to help her up from the bed of hay. "You sure it's Amsterdam that has you sore and not me?"

She couldn't help the blush that spread across her features. She'd been married to this man for over ten years, yet he could still do this to her. "Now that you mention it…"

He pulled her to him when she was on her feet and wrapped his arms around her waist. Her chest was pressed against his solid one, which was drenched in perspiration. "I hope you weren't teasing about finding that pool of water."

He held her gaze. "I kid you not. When was the last time we went swimming together alone?"

"In case you've forgotten, I believe that's how I got pregnant with Tatum." She studied his features to see if her reminder would squash the desire she saw in his eyes. It didn't. In fact, she could feel the lower part of his body harden.

To further confuse her, he smiled. "I remember now. The folks kept Tia so you could join me that time in Germany."

So, he had remembered his R and R time, when he'd rented a house with a pool. She had stayed two weeks. When she'd left, she was pregnant. They had hoped for that, thinking it was time for Tia to have a sibling.

"Now we work out," she said, trying to ease from his arms.

"Not yet. I haven't kissed you good-morning yet. Do you have any idea how often I wake up whenever I'm on an operation, wishing it was your face I was waking up to see, and not my teammates'. I would give anything to be able to kiss you when it's a real kiss and not a dream. So, Teri McRoy, I hope you don't mind indulging me right now."

She swallowed while gazing up at him. They were supposed to talk this morning. She knew that. But a kiss, exercise and a swim sounded a whole lot better.

For now.

"Not at all, Mac, as long as you promise that's all it will be, a kiss."

As he lowered his head to her lips, he whispered, "I promise."

Nine

Mac was convinced he could stand there and kiss his wife forever since he enjoyed doing it just that much. He intended to make sure she enjoyed it, as well, and from the way she was kissing him back, she was.

It was times like these when he missed her the most. Times like these when he regretted being away from her and the girls as much and as often as he was. Losing the baby had been hard on her, and he of all people knew it. A part of him knew she was still going through a grieving period, a period he'd yet to share with her.

Yet, he grieved regardless. For the son he'd lost and for the wife a part of him felt he was losing.

His concentration was pulled back to her when she began wiggling her tongue all around in his mouth, something he had taught her to do years ago. It was during those times when pleasuring him was the only thing she wanted to do, and he'd been all in.

But not now. Although it might kill him, he would keep his promise. If nothing else, he now understood what she needed and he knew what he needed. There were a number of issues on the table. First and foremost, he needed to prove to his wife that she mattered. If he had made the mistake of taking her for granted, taking their marriage for granted, it was time he shaped up or shipped out. Mac had no intentions of calling it quits where his wife and family were concerned. He needed them as much as he wanted them to need him.

He reluctantly broke off the kiss and pulled his mouth back. He had to take control, both mentally and physically…especially physically. He couldn't take care of the latter until they wrapped themselves around the problems that could eventually destroy their marriage if they went unchecked.

His wife could be pregnant. He knew how she felt about that possibility because he'd asked, and she'd had no problem telling him. The one thing she hadn't asked was how he felt about it. Why? Did she think he wouldn't feel the same way?

He knew they had a lot of emotions to deal with. They were emotions he had conditioned himself not to feel.

But not anymore.

"Come on, time to join me and work out."

"You did good, kiddo."

Totally out of breath and bending over with hands resting on her knees, Teri glanced up at Mac. "Thanks. Glad you approve." She'd worked out in moderation. It was too early to tell if she was pregnant but just in case, she'd decided not to overdo anything. "I'm ready for my swim now."

"Then come with me." He took her hand in

his and she tried not to think about how good it felt whenever he did that.

They didn't say anything and she wondered what he was thinking. He hadn't put his jeans and shirt back on but seemed perfectly at ease to walk through the mineshaft in just his briefs and carrying his clothes in one hand while holding her hand with the other.

Glancing down, he asked, "How did you sleep last night?"

She smiled up at him. "Great. You kept me warm and I appreciated that. You took good care of me, Mac."

"And I always will."

For some reason his words touched her. Now if she could only get him to believe in her. But then, was she being fair wanting him to do that when she hadn't been totally forthcoming with him about what she'd done? She still had the issue of her buying the ranch between them. She still intended to tell him about it today like she had promised. But she wanted to find the right time to do so.

"So what do you think?"

She glanced up and saw the inlet, a small

pool of crystal clear water. This was better than she expected. "How is this possible?" she turned to asked him.

"I figure it's part of that lake we saw a mile or so back and is a spill-off running underground. Because the water is warm, it must be connected to a hot spring, as well. I checked it out to make sure it's not a whirlpool. It doesn't look deep. You can swim, so you'll be fine."

Yes, she could swim. There had been a number of swimming holes on her grandparents' ranch. "Are you swimming, as well?" she asked, unbuttoning her shirt. She paused and glanced over at him upon realizing what she was doing. She was about to strip in front of him. He was her husband, so honestly, there shouldn't be an issue in her doing that. But there was. Could she honestly expect him not to touch her if he saw her naked? She'd never placed restrictions or limitations on their lovemaking before.

She looked over at him. "Mac?"

"Go ahead and take off your clothes, Teri. I understood what you said about us not making love until we get some issues in our marriage resolved. I won't touch you, no matter what. I do have control, you know."

Yes, she knew about his control, but he'd never had to exercise restraint when it came to her. She nodded and then, while he watched, she stripped down to her bra and panties.

She glanced over at him, saw the heat in his gaze. He gave her one of his sexy smiles and said, "Maybe I shouldn't have encouraged you to remove your clothes after all."

She returned his smile. "Too late to call it back now."

He shrugged massive shoulders before shoving away from the wall to move toward her. "I guess so. Come on, let's swim."

When they got close to the water, they dived in.

As Mac watched Teri glide through the water, he realized he had forgotten just what a skilled swimmer she was. She looked good and he was fighting every part of his desirous body. He'd done several laps and now just preferred hanging back while she did hers.

Her body was perfectly arched as she progressed through the water, moving her head from side to side as she concentrated on her strokes.

It dawned on him then how relaxed she appeared, so carefree. Today she didn't have to be the mommy in control or the wife in demand. She could be Teri. It had been years since he'd seen her this...at peace. It was then he blamed himself for a lot of things. For not recognizing that she needed downtime. As her husband he should have taken her away somewhere, and often. Just the two of them.

They could have not only stimulated their minds but talked about a lot of things that bothered them. Parents needed "me" time, and he could see that now. She'd held a part-time job at a library for a couple of years now and he'd never even asked how she liked it. Mainly because he hadn't wanted her to work. He now saw just how unfair that was to her.

"I enjoyed that, Mac."

He blinked, realizing Teri had swum over to him. He'd been so caught up in his thoughts that he hadn't noticed her approach. "I'm glad you did." He pulled himself up over the edge and then reached his hand to help her out, as well.

"Thanks."

"You're welcome." He stepped back since standing too close to her could affect his self-control. "No towels, so we'll have to air our bodies dry."

"And risk catching pneumonia?" she asked, ringing the water out of her hair. "Do this."

He lifted a brow. "Do what?"

"This." She then demonstrated using her hands to wipe off excess water from her body and doing it in such a way that her palms appeared to act as a sponge.

Mac doubted Teri had any idea how turned on he was getting just watching her rub her hands all over herself. It was a definite turn-on, which was something he could do without right now. Not to call attention to his growing erection, he followed her lead and saw her technique was working. "How do you know about this?"

She chuckled. "Nothing top secret here. Just one of those 'mommy knows it all' things."

"I see." And in a way, he was at least beginning to see. It wasn't that he hadn't appreciated her role as the mother of his kids before because he had. However, he would admit he'd never been privy to those 'mommy things' and just how good she was at them before now.

He didn't say anything as they put their clothes back on and he didn't try to be discreet in watching her.

He'd said he wouldn't touch her; he hadn't promised he wouldn't get his fill of admiring how her body looked.

"I'm hungry now."

He smiled. "Tuna and water again. This time with peaches."

"I'll take it. My grandparents used to say beggars can't be choosers."

He laughed. "That's funny. My parents would often say the same thing. Come on, let's eat."

Sheriff Corilla smiled appreciatively. "I can't thank you men enough for what you did. I doubt little Larry Johnson will be wandering off again anytime soon."

"We were glad to help, Sheriff," Bane said.

The little boy had been found alive and well, although hungry, and had been returned to his parents. "Now we could use your help."

"Certainly. What can I do?"

"This is our former SEAL team member, Nick Stover. He was able to pinpoint Mac's location."

Sheriff Corilla lifted a brow. "You did?" he asked, shaking Nick's hand.

Nick nodded. "Yes, and that's where I need your help," he said, clicking on his laptop, which immediately flared to life. Within seconds an aerial view came on the screen. "Based on the latitude, longitude and altitude I've documented, Mac's location has been pinpointed to this area."

"Information you've documented?" Corilla asked, rubbing his chin. It was obvious he was trying to figure out just how Nick had managed that. But they figured he knew it was something for which he wouldn't be getting answers, so he turned his attention to the laptop screen.

"That's Martinsville," he said. "It's a mining site that's been deserted for over five years now. I had my men check out the area and they said the tornado ripped through there pretty bad. Since the place has been deserted we had no reason to hang around."

"Evidently Mac and Teri were in the area and sought refuge in one of those mineshafts. That's where we're headed," Coop said.

"We figure there's a lot of debris in the area, so my four brothers are on their way with heavy equipment and machinery to help plow our way through," Flipper added.

Sheriff Corilla nodded. "You're going to need it. There are three shafts there, within several feet of each other. And according to my men, the windmill came down in that area and several trees were uprooted and landed on them, as well. I don't know which one your friend and his wife might be holed up inside, but I'm hoping it's not this one," he said, pointing at the mineshaft on the right.

"Why?" Viper asked.

Sheriff Corilla glanced over at him. "It contains a pool of water, a hot spring, so to speak."

Bane lifted a brow. "We have several of

those on my property in Denver. Why would that pose a threat?"

"Because it's a spill-off from McKevor Lake and I understand that the runoff from the lake is blocked with fallen trees and limbs acting like a dam, impeding natural flow. That means the water has nowhere to go."

Nick stared at the sheriff. "You believe there will be flooding in the area?"

"Yes, and it's already started. But what causes grave concern with this particular mineshaft is that because of the spring inside, it will start flooding when the spring over-flows, with no warning. Unfortunately, there is no high section within the mineshaft to es-cape the rising water. It's happened before, and a couple of unsuspecting miners lost their lives. If you honestly think this is where the McRoys are, then I suggest you get them out as soon as possible."

Ten

"Tell me about your job at that library, Teri."

She glanced over at Mac, wondering why he wanted to know more about it when her working there had been a sore point with him. Besides, he'd never before asked her about what she did at the library. Was this his lead-in question before they argued about her keeping her job?

"What do you want to know about it?"

"Anything you want to tell me."

Honestly? Did he? There was only one way to find out. "I only work three days a week, four hours a day, but I love what I do."

"Which is?"

"I'm in charge of the history section. That's great for me because of my degree in history. I get to suggest good books to the people who come to the library, about whatever part of history they are interested in. You won't believe the number of young people who come to the library wanting books on the World Wars, specifically World War II."

"Why do you think that is?"

"Not sure, but I'm just glad they are interested in it. I believe you can't fully appreciate your present until you know your past. At least that's what's my granddad used to say."

"I wish I could have met your grandparents. They sound like swell people."

He'd told her that several times before, when she'd told him something her grandparents had passed on to her. "And there's no doubt they would have wanted to meet you." Sadly, her mother had died when she'd been two and her father before her tenth birthday, leaving her to be raised by her grandparents.

They had been the best and when they'd died not long after she'd finished college, within the same year, it had been hard for her. Selling the ranch they'd loved had been even harder and a part of her felt she'd let them down by doing so. Now she owned it again. Would Mac understand her need to atone for those feelings of guilt? Would he understand that was one of her reasons for doing what she'd done?

"I'm glad you're doing something that you enjoy, Teri."

She looked over at him. Did he really? If he did, then that was a switch. "Why, Mac? Why are you glad now when you've always been resentful?"

"I've never been resentful, not really. I just never understood your need to work outside the home."

"And you do now?" she asked, staring at him.

He nodded. "Yes, I'm beginning to. In a way, it's no different than my need to do something I love. I wanted to be a SEAL since listening to my maternal grandfather tell me of all the things he did as one. I wanted that kind of life. The adventure. The need to protect my country. Mom and Dad didn't understand why I would pass on a football scholarship to apply to the naval academy instead."

He didn't say anything for a minute and then added, "The only other thing I needed to make my life complete was something I thought I'd never find, and that was a mate who was willing to put up with it. But then I found you. However, in creating the life I wanted, I failed to realize something."

"What?"

He studied her for a moment. "That you had dreams of your own. Dreams I expected you to forgo for mine."

Teri didn't say anything, realizing this was the first time they'd had a heart-to-heart talk on things that bothered her and that had affected their marriage. Yes, they'd sought counseling, but even then she'd felt Mac had never given those sessions his absolute all. He'd merely been placating her at the time.

"And do you know what's obvious to me now, Teri?"

"No, what?"

"That you did forgo them. And instead of appreciating your sacrifice, I scorned you every time I returned from a mission for decisions you made in my absence."

Teri couldn't let him take full blame. There were some decisions she could have given more in-depth thought to before making them. But then there were some decisions, like the purchase of the ranch, that, although made on the spur of the moment, had been a dream come true for her.

"It wasn't always that way, Mac. Even I admit there were some things I could have done differently." She paused. It was time to tell him about the ranch. She'd withheld it from him long enough. "Mac, I—"

"Wait," he said, holding up his hand. She saw his body go on full alert as he glanced around.

She glanced around, as well, wondering what had drawn his attention but knew now was not the time to ask. He was in his "ready to act" mode.

"You hear that?" he suddenly asked, quickly coming to his feet and placing his tuna can aside.

She strained her ears. "No, I don't hear anything. What do you hear?"

He looked at her. "Rushing water. Stay here." He quickly walked off.

Rushing water?

She didn't like the sound of that. Suddenly an eerie feeling passed through her. No, she wouldn't stay here. She stood, put her own tuna can aside and went after Mac.

Bane Westmoreland glanced around at what used to be a mining site. It had taken a full two hours to cut through downed trees and plow through all kinds of debris to get there. He appreciated one of Flipper's brothers for having the mind to bring several bulldozers. If it hadn't been for that equipment, they would still be miles away from here.

That tornado had done more damage than they'd thought. Since this was uninhabited land, the devastation in this section of Torchlight hadn't made the news. Nick had decisively pinpointed the mineshaft that Mac was holed up in as the one with the spill-off. Even though they didn't have concrete proof, they figured he and Teri were together. Getting them out safely from among all this rubble would be a challenge but they intended to do it.

According to Nick, who was monitoring Mac's tracker, he'd been pretty active this morning. From the timing and frequency of Mac's movements they'd concluded he'd been working out. Not surprising, since Mac could be anal when it came to fitness.

"I checked on him twenty minutes ago and he was in a relax mode," Nick was saying to them now.

"That means he hadn't detected anything," Coop surmised.

"That was twenty minutes ago, and he might have figured it out by now," Viper chimed in to say. "We need to get them out. We've seen that lake and the water has to go somewhere. Since it's not flooding aboveground, that means it will be flooding connecting outlets below. Mac has no idea that's going to happen."

"Or no way to stop it when it does," Flipper added.

Bane, like the others, knew the seriousness of what was about to happen. He was about to say something when Nick interrupted. "Hey, guys, I just got a new reading on Mac. He's on the move and his brain waves are signaling trouble."

Bane nodded, his expression serious. "Okay, guys, let's get Mac and Teri out of there and send them home to their girls."

Mac rushed quickly to where the pool was located and got halfway when the sound of rushing water increased. When he got to where the troughs of hay had been, he stopped. There was standing water in that area. "What the hell!"

He quickly moved past the troughs and when he stepped on what had been a solid floor, suddenly the board beneath him collapsed. He broke the fall by grabbing hold of a boulder, the same one he'd sat on that morning. Gripping tightly, he barely held on. There was no doubt in his mind that if he fell he would get swept away in the rushing water below.

"Mac!"

He snatched his head upward and saw Teri coming toward him. Hadn't he told her to stay put?

"Go back, Teri. There's a chance the floor might collapse under you. Water is flooding the mineshaft. You need to go back and find a high place and stay there."

"And leave you here?"

"Yes."

She frowned at him. "Not on your life, Thurston McRoy!"

"Teri…" he said in a warning tone. "Please do as I say."

"Save your breath," she said, glancing around. "Hold on, Mac. I've got an idea."

She had an idea? What kind of idea could she have? Teri needed to get her butt out of there and try to find higher ground, although he didn't recall there being any higher ground. The thought of anything happening to her had him—

Suddenly Mac felt a rope tossed around him. He glanced up and watched Teri reviving her role as a cowgirl. Twirling the rope around the air in perfect precision, she then lassoed him in with a second rope that went around his body perfectly.

Ropes? What in the world? Where did those ropes come from?

"Pull yourself out now, Mac!"

He tugged upward and found it was tight. Where had she tied the end of the rope for it to be as sturdy as it was? Knowing the answer would come soon enough, he used the rope to hoist himself back up on solid ground.

"Mac!" Teri threw herself into his arms and he held on to her tight. "I thought I was going to lose you."

He then pulled back but kept his arms around her waist. "Thanks, but I told you to stay back."

She lifted her chin. "And I disobeyed. Good thing I did."

"Where did the ropes come from?"

"Some troughs are built with a compartment underneath to hold a rope. I checked and they were there. I hadn't lassoed in a while but knew I had to do it. I tied the ends around the trough to take your weight when you pulled yourself up." She glanced around and saw the flooding waters. "What is going on?"

"Looks like the lake is flooding with the spill-off, which means we need to find higher ground."

"Is there higher ground in here?"

He had been afraid she would ask that. He took her hand when more water began flowing in around them at a high rate of speed. "Come on. If there is, we need to find it."

They were trying to outrun the water and Teri saw they couldn't. Already the water was waist-deep and just as she'd feared, there was no higher ground. She wouldn't get hysterical, but they were going to die.

At least the girls were in good hands and she and Mac were together.

He'd stopped and was looking around and she knew without him saying that there was nowhere else to go. They were back where they started, which was at the entrance, but nothing had changed and it was still blocked.

He was still holding her hand and she tightened her hold on his. "Mac, I love you and you've been a good husband, and—"

"We will be rescued, Teri," he interrupted her to say.

She lifted a brow. "By who?"

"The guys."

She knew what guys he was talking about. His teammates. Did he really believe that? Or in their last moments of life was he trying to give her hope? "How will they rescue us, Mac?"

He shrugged as he looked at the blocked opening. "Not sure how, but they will get it done. In the meantime, I need you to stand on my shoulders."

"What? Why?"

"Because that will keep the water from getting to you until they do."

She frowned, knowing that meant the water would get to him first. "And what about you?"

"Don't worry about me. Timing is important. We could tread water, but not for long. If the guys can't save us both, at least they will have more time to save you. Now, let me hoist you up on my shoulders."

She shook her head, imagining the weight of her on his shoulders with water steadily surrounding them. "No, I won't do it."

"Don't argue with me," he said, trying to lift her up.

She pushed his hands away, although already the water was nearly up to her breasts. However, she didn't care. She would not have him risk his life to save hers. "Mac, please don't ask me to do that. What will I tell the girls?"

He reached out and caressed her cheek. "The same thing we agreed long ago to tell them if I never returned home. That I love them and will always love them. Just so you know, the same applies to their mother, as well. I love you."

Mac leaned down to kiss her. She knew it was supposed to be a brush of his lips against hers but the moment their lips touched, their passions were inflamed. It didn't matter that water was still increasing around them. Nothing mattered but this kiss and she refused to believe this was their last.

Mac finally broke off the kiss and whispered against moist lips, "And if you are pregnant,

Teri, please let our son or daughter know I would have welcomed them into our world with all the love a father could give."

She fought back her tears. "Don't do this to me, Mac. You just said that your teammates are coming. Are you now doubting their abilities?"

"No. They are SEALs. They just might not have enough time to save us both and you are more important."

"Says who?"

"Says me." Then, in an unexpected move, he quickly pulled her up to sit upon his shoulders. She tried struggling free and he said, "Stay put or you'll knock me off-balance and we'll both drown."

"Don't do this, Mac. Let me down."

"No."

Mac was six-foot-three and water had already reached the upper part of his chest. Had she remained standing beside him, it would be up to her neck now.

It seemed the water was coming in faster and when she felt her backside get wet she knew the water was up to Mac's shoulders.

Tears she couldn't hold back anymore began to flow.

Then suddenly, when she knew the water was close to Mac's neck, she heard him laugh out loud and say, "About time."

She glanced down from her place perched on Mac's shoulders to see one of his teammates. Flipper. Where had he come from?

"Whatever," Flipper said. "Stop being an unappreciative ass." He then glanced up at her and smiled. "Hi, Teri," he greeted, like it was a normal thing to find them trapped in a mineshaft that was quickly filling with water.

"How did you get in here?" she asked, needing to know. Mac had said they would be coming, but honestly, she truly hadn't believed him.

"We figured it would take longer to remove all the debris from the entrance, so they made an opening large enough for me to swim through," Flipper explained. "We need to hurry up and leave out the same way. Here," he said, handing her a snorkel mask and then giving Mac one, as well.

"Where is yours?" she asked him.

He gave her an arrogant smile, his blue eyes flashing. "I don't need one. Now quickly put it on."

Teri did as he said, remembering Mac's claim that Flipper, master diver, could hold his breath underwater longer than any human he knew.

"You can release Teri off your shoulders now, Mac, to put on your mask." The water was close to Mac's face and he reluctantly released her to Flipper so he could put on his mask.

"I will lead you guys out. Follow me. We need to be careful. Some of the pieces of debris floating around in the water have jagged edges."

Flipper dived into the water, and Mac motioned for Teri to follow. She dived in behind Flipper, knowing Mac was bringing up the rear.

Eleven

"I am so glad to see you guys," Mac said to his friends. He was surprised to see Nick as well as Flipper's four SEAL brothers. "I had no idea that the mine would flood."

"We didn't, either," Bane said, grateful their mission had been accomplished and Mac and Teri were safe.

"Had we known we would have rescued you sooner. We've been here for two days," Coop added.

Mac lifted a brow. "Two days? Then what took you guys so long?" he asked.

Viper's shoulder lifted in a careless shrug.

"We assisted the sheriff in finding a little boy. That took an entire day. Besides, your brain waves were signaling you were in a pretty calm state, so we figured you and Teri could use that time to work out a few issues."

"Oh, you did, did you?" Mac said, frowning deeply.

"Yes, we did," Bane replied. "When we talked to you the day you got here you were in a foul mood, already eating nails, shooting fire and ready to give your wife hell. We were hoping the time alone would help. Did it?"

Mac glanced over at his wife, who was being checked by one of the first responders. Damn, he loved that woman. She'd been a real trouper and he could credit her with saving his life. He looked back at his friends. "Yes, but it will be an ongoing process, guys. I admit I'm seeing things in a different light, but…"

"You'll still resort to being an ass when the mood suits you," Viper said, frowning.

Mac gave Viper a daggered look. "You act like I enjoy being difficult."

"Don't you?" Coop asked. "You've had

plenty of time to clean up your act and accept Teri as your equal."

"I do accept her as my equal. Damn it, she saved my life in that mine," he snapped out.

Surprise and shock appeared on his friends' faces. "She did?"

"Yes." He then told them what happened.

"Wow," Flipper said. "It's a good thing you married a cowgirl with smarts. Some people would have freaked out."

Mac nodded. "Teri has a level head on her shoulders."

"She just doesn't know how to spend your money, right?"

Instead of waiting for his answer, his friends walked off.

Out of the corner of her eye, Teri had watched Mac talk to his friends. Even across the distance, she could feel the closeness he had with them was unlike what he had with her. Of course, it would be different since they were his friends and she was his wife, but he trusted them unequivocally. He trusted her but with conditions.

She appreciated their time together in the mineshaft. They'd ironed out a number of things that had been eroding their marriage. But they still had work to do. She still had confessions to make. And she believed they would do that work because they loved each other and neither of them wanted what they had to end.

Teri knew she still had to tell him about the ranch. She had been about to tell him when he'd detected something was wrong. Now she had to find time to discuss it with him. Right now, she was just glad they'd been rescued. She was ready to go home to their girls.

First thing she wanted to do was check into a hotel and take a good bath and wash her hair. They'd been told the cabin had been destroyed and they would be allowed to go look through the rubble to recover any of their belongings. Then there was the issue of more clothes, which meant she and Mac needed to go shopping.

For now, she didn't want her husband out of her sight. She'd come close to losing him. They'd come close to losing each other and she was still having a hard time getting beyond that fact.

"You're free to go now, Ms. McRoy."

She glanced up at the first responder, who'd been treating the minor cuts on her arm from a piece of debris. "Thanks."

She stood and glanced back over at Mac. He was now standing alone and looking at her and doing so in such a way she could feel heat stir in the bottom of her stomach. No matter what, they had shared an experience in that mineshaft that would always be there, unifying them, bonding them.

She broke eye contact with him and looked down at herself. She'd been given a blanket. His clothes were still wet and so were hers. They'd also been told the vehicles they'd driven to the ranch had been totaled. More bad news. The main ranch house had sustained a lot of damage and was now uninhabitable. But the good news was that Amsterdam and the other horse had survived the tornado. She'd been glad to hear that.

"Ready to go to the hotel?"

She looked at the man with the deep, husky voice. Her husband. "How will we leave?"

He held up a key fob. "Bane left us his rental. I figured we could go get cleaned up, buy new clothes and then return to the cabin to see what we can recover. However, I have a feeling a lot of the stuff is lost."

She had a similar feeling about that. Luckily, she'd only brought a few things with her. "What about your things?"

He shrugged. "All replaceable. Ready?"

She nodded. "Yes, I'm ready." She had already thanked Mac's teammates but wanted to thank them again. She looked round and didn't see them anywhere. "Where did the guys go?"

"They're on their way back home."

She could understand that. Like Mac they'd returned to their homes only a few days ago from their last operation. Yet they'd left their families to come here to save her and Mac. And they *had* saved them. She and Mac had been just minutes away from drowning.

"I really appreciated what they did, Mac. You are part of a wonderful team." Teri figured he already knew that but wanted to speak the obvious anyway.

"Yes, I am."

From Mac's expression Teri could tell he, too, was filled with deep gratitude. They knew what the outcome would have been if Mac's SEAL team hadn't arrived when they had. And then for Nick Stovers and Flipper's brothers to be included in the mix was super special. She truly appreciated everyone's help.

"Yes, I'm ready to leave. I need a bath and my hair needs washing."

"I'll take care of both for you. Come on." He took her hand and headed toward the waiting SUV.

Mac glanced over at his wife as he backed the vehicle out of the parking lot. Her eyes were closed and he figured it wouldn't be long before she was asleep. She deserved to rest and he would be the first to say she'd been more than a great trouper. She'd been a real life-saver. It was something he would never forget. His gut tightened at the thought of how she'd put her own life on the line. She had kept a level head and done what she needed to do.

His friends had given him food for thought. But he'd been doing a lot of thinking long before they'd fed him any words. The problems in his marriage wouldn't disappear with just a few days holed up in a mineshaft. It would take continuous work on their part. Especially on his.

"Mac..."

He glanced over at Teri when she said his name. She'd fallen asleep, so in sleep she was thinking about him. Such a thing touched him deeply. While at the hotel he intended to pamper her. What he hadn't told her was that thanks to the wives of his teammates, certain arrangements had already been made.

A smile touched his lips. He needed more time with his wife and intended to get all the time he could. They would be returning home to Virginia soon.

When he stopped at a traffic light, he turned to look at her and saw how her head was resting against the back of the seat. Hair had fallen in her face and he couldn't resist the temptation to reach out and brush a few dark curls back from her forehead. He didn't stop there. The pad of his finger gently rubbed against her cheek. His action didn't wake her, didn't even make her stir. Instead she continued to sleep.

He had a stop or two to make before they got to the hotel, one place in particular.

"We're here, Teri."

Teri slowly opened her eyes. Yawning, she pulled up in her seat and looked through the car's window. "Where are we?"

"At a hotel in Cheyenne. All the ones in Torchlight were filled to capacity with so many first responders arriving. They still have a lot of people unaccounted for."

"I hope they find them. That first responder who treated me told me how your teammates helped find a little boy. That was special." Easing her seat belt from around her waist, she asked, "Are you sure we can get a room here? The place looks full, if the parking lot is any indication."

"Don't worry, we have a room."

Teri glanced over at him. Something about

his words sent heat flowing through her. They had a room? It wasn't what he'd said but how he'd said it that made certain areas within her stir. "Good."

"Stay put. I'll be around to open the door for you, Teri."

Last time he'd given her such an order she'd defied him, but not this time. She was too tired to move just yet. Swimming out of that mine hadn't been easy and she had been grateful for Flipper being in front of her and Mac at the rear. Paramedics had been there to check them over the moment they'd reached solid ground. In less than five minutes after they'd gotten out, the sheriff announced the mineshaft was filled with water from top to bottom and she'd known there was no way she and Mac would have survived.

"Do you need me to carry you inside?"

She glanced up at Mac. He'd come around the side of the car and opened the door for her. He had a store bag in his hand. "No, I can walk. You made a stop somewhere?" she asked. He reached out and circled her wrist with his long fingers. He was wearing another

Stetson and she wondered where he'd gotten it when the one he'd purchased the day he'd arrived had been destroyed in the flood.

Mac smiled. "Yes, I made a couple of stops. You slept through them."

"Oh. I guess I was more exhausted than I thought."

"You've been through a lot, Teri."

She glanced over at him as they walked inside the hotel. "We both have."

Teri noted that instead of checking in at the front desk, Mac led her over to the bank of elevators. It was a beautiful hotel, one of the well-known chains. The lobby was filled with a lot of fresh flowers. She didn't know how long they'd driven to get here. This hotel wasn't located in downtown Cheyenne but on the outskirts of town.

"We don't have to check in?"

He looked down at her when they stepped inside the elevator. "No. The guys took care of it."

She wondered what else the guys had taken care of and found out when they reached their hotel room. A bottle of champagne was on ice with a card that said Compliments of Team Six. There was also a huge bag from the hotel's gift shop and another bag from a well-known clothing store in the middle of the king-size bed.

"What's this?" she asked, moving toward the bed. Although the hotel room wasn't a suite, she thought it was larger than most. It even had a small balcony instead of just a window. They were on the tenth floor and the balcony overlooked some of the most beautiful valleys and meadows she'd ever seen.

"Clothes that my teammates' wives ordered for you from a clothing store downtown. I told them what we needed and the sizes. The guys ordered clothes for me from one of those western outfitters in town. They picked everything up and delivered it here before heading out to the airport."

"Who? Your teammates?"

"Yes, thank God for online shopping."

Teri was touched by what everyone had done. His teammates and their wives. Women she'd gotten to know. "That was truly nice of them, Mac."

"Yes, it was." He tossed the bags he was carrying on the bed to join the others. "Now for your bath. You prefer the tub or a shower?"

"The shower will be fine. That way I can wash my hair." She went through one of the bags and pulled out a pair of jeans and a Western shirt. There were also underthings—bra and panties. She also had more boots and another hat. She looked at the tags on the clothing. Of course they were her size. When it came to her, Mac knew every single physical detail.

She glanced over at him. "You did good in telling them what I needed."

"I try. Now go ahead and get started on your shower. I have an important call to make and I'll be in there in a minute."

He would be in there in a minute? Did that mean he planned to join her in her shower? It wouldn't be the first time if he did, so why did the thought of him doing such a thing arouse her with anticipation?

"Oh, okay." She grabbed the underthings from the bag and quickly headed for the bathroom.

Twelve

Mac hung up the phone after ordering room service from the hotel's restaurant to be delivered in a few hours. He and Teri needed to go back to the cabin, search through the rubble to see if they could recover any of their belongings. But not today. They had more urgent and pressing business to attend to.

Going over to the nightstand, he pulled open the drawer to retrieve the bag he'd kept separate from the others. Pulling out one of several condom packets, he headed for the bathroom.

The room was steamy and although he couldn't see her, he knew Teri was somewhere behind the opaque glass wall. He placed the condom on the vanity before stripping off his clothes. Reclaiming the packet, he moved toward the shower door. All he could think of was a naked Teri, that fine body of hers and how much he needed to sink into it.

When he opened the door, she had her back to him with her head under the sprayer as she washed her hair. But the swoosh of air as the door opened must've alerted her that she was no longer alone. He saw her body tense and go still.

"Mac?"

"Who else would it be?" he asked, placing the condom packet in the soap compartment before easing up behind her.

She relaxed her body against his. "Can't ever be too sure. I've watched enough *NCIS* to reach that conclusion."

He started to tell her that was television fabricated for her enjoyment and then decided not to bother. If watching those shows kept her cautious whenever he was gone, then so be it. "Then rest assured it's me, baby," he said, bringing her body back against him and leaning close to whisper in her ear.

"Okay, it's you. I thought we decided we wouldn't do this."

"Because you're not on any birth control," he said, using the tip of his tongue to lick against the side of her ear.

"Yes, and we need to reach an understanding in our marriage."

He pushed the wet hair from her face after he turned her around to look at him. "Taking you or our marriage for granted is something I've never wanted to do, Teri, and if I did do that, then I'm sorry. I do understand your feelings, trust your decisions, respect what you do while I'm gone. I will get better but don't expect me to change overnight. Please accept me as 'work in progress.' I promise to do better but I'm human, I might make mistakes along the way."

"I'm human, too, and I might make mistakes, as well, Mac."

"Good, now we understand each other and agree to work together to improve our marriage."

"Yes, but I need to tell you what I bought while you were gone. You're not going to like it."

"It doesn't matter this time. Considering what you've gone through, what we've both gone through, it doesn't matter to me now. Whatever it is you bought without talking it over with me, I'll forgive you for it this time. Consider it a pardon."

She raised a brow. "A pardon?"

"Yes. Everyone is entitled to at least one during their lifetime."

"But you don't know what I bought or the cost."

He shrugged as he reached above her head for the shampoo. "Doesn't matter. We still have a roof over our head and food to eat, right?"

"Yes."

"Then whatever you bought didn't put us in the poorhouse."

"You sure, Mac?"

"Positive. And you can tell me all about it later. Better yet, surprise me."

"Surprise you?"

"Yes. Surprise me. Right now, the only thing I want to think about is doing other things."

"Other things like what?"

"Making love to my wife. And don't worry. I stopped by a store to grab a few condoms." There was no need to tell her he'd gotten the economy pack of a dozen.

She smiled up at him. "Why aren't I surprised?"

"Not sure. Why aren't you?"

Instead of answering him she raised up on tiptoe, wrapped her arms around his neck and pressed her mouth against his.

Joy filled Teri.

Mac was giving her a pardon. That meant even if he hadn't agreed with her purchase of the ranch, this time he wouldn't make a big deal out of it. But still, she knew moving forward he had to agree to trust her more to handle things when he was gone. They would both be works in progress and she didn't have a problem with that.

He broke off the kiss and reached up to fill his hands with shampoo from the dispenser.

"Turn around. I know you've already lathered your hair but I want to do it again. I love washing your hair."

She turned her back to him and sighed deeply at the feel of his fingers working lather into her scalp. That, coupled with her backside resting against his groin, sent a multitude of sensations all through her.

Teri was convinced nobody could wash her hair the way Mac did. He had the best fingers…for everything. She recalled those same fingers touching every part of her body, especially when he worked those same fingers inside her, making her reach an orgasm of gigantic proportions.

"You like the way that feels, baby?"

"Hmm," she said, not able to say the words, yet knowing he knew what she meant.

"Now for the rinse-out."

He tilted her head back under the spray and she felt warm water rushing through her hair and down her back. After squeezing excess water from her head, he said, "Now to clean the rest of you."

Then, filling his hands with soap, he used

his hands to lather her body. The feel of his hands on her body made her moan because he knew exactly what areas to touch.

"You shouldn't stir me this way, Mac," she said, when he turned her around to face him.

"Why not?"

Did he really have to ask her that? "I can't think straight when you do."

He began lathering her front and said, "It wouldn't bother me in the least if you were to stop thinking at all. Or if you think only about me."

Little did he know she did that anyway. He didn't know how lonely her nights were without him in bed with her. "How can you be so sexy and so annoying at the same time?"

"It's a gift, babe," he leaned in and whispered before placing a kiss across her lips.

Then, using the sprayer, he washed the suds from her body and then ran his hands all over her. "You're squeaky-clean now."

She believed him. He had washed her hair and her body. "Now for me to wash you."

Lathering her hands with soap, she began rubbing them all over his body. Her husband

was well-endowed and his erection was showing her how loaded he was. Touching him
made sensations flood her insides, made a tingling sensation settle between her thighs. No
part of his body missed her care and attention.

When she heard him moan, she glanced up
and met his gaze. Held it and felt desire and
love in the very depths of her soul. Holding
him in her hand always did this to her, em-
powered her as a woman.

His woman.

"You're killing me, you know."

She shook her head and smiled. "You're a
SEAL. I heard they don't die easily. They're
too rough and tough."

"Then why do I feel like putty in your hands?"

Teri threw her head back and laughed as she
continued to hold him. "Trust me, this does
not feel like putty. Not one single inch of it."

After figuring she'd tortured him enough,
she used the sprayer to wash all the suds from
his body. No sooner had she done that than
he suddenly backed her against the shower
stall. "Now I'm going to take care of you, Teri
Anne."

"You always take care of me, Thurston."

He smiled and she watched him retrieve the condom packet from where he'd placed it earlier. He made quick work of sheathing himself. Returning to her, he asked, "Now, where was I?"

"If you have to ask, then maybe we—"

He didn't give her a chance to finish. Mac lifted her onto him at the same time he captured her mouth in his. And when he began thrusting hard into her, Teri was convinced that, considering his ferocious sexual appetite, he intended to make up for lost time.

Thirteen

Mac opened his eyes to find Teri sitting cross-legged in the middle of the bed, staring at him. Seeing her flooded his mind with memories of how they'd spent the last few hours. They had made love in the shower, dried off and made love again in the bed. Dinner had arrived in their room and afterward they'd taken a walk outside only to return to their hotel room to make love again. All night long.

It was morning and the sun was shining brightly through the window shades. It was a beautiful day and he had awakened to the face of an even more beautiful woman. A woman sitting in the middle of the bed with a huge grin on her face. A stunning smile. It was even a mischievous smile. For a minute, she looked like the cat that ate the canary.

"Good morning, Mac."

Instead of responding, he reached out and cupped his hands behind her head to bring her face closer to his. And then he did something that he'd done a lot of lately. He kissed her, getting the feel of her that he definitely needed.

It was strange how things worked out. He'd left Virginia to come after his wife. There began an adventure, one he could certainly have done without, but possibly one that was needed. He couldn't recall when the two of them had spent so much "us" time together. They missed their girls, he knew that, but they were enjoying the time they were spending here with each other. He and Teri would return to the cabin to go through the rubble and sometime later today they would be returning home.

By the time the kiss ended, he was ready to pull her deeper into his arms for another kiss, but she pulled back and said, still smiling brightly, "Today you get your surprise."

He lifted a brow as he reached out and gently rubbed up and down her arm, needing the contact and loving the feel of her smooth skin. "My surprise?"

Her smile got even brighter. "Yes. I've made all the arrangements."

He was trying to keep up with her but failing. "What arrangements, sweetheart?"

"To take you to see your surprise. Mac, please keep up," she said jokingly.

He was trying. He leaned up and kissed her again, this one just as thorough but not as long. "I'm trying. How about you start from the beginning since I'm sure there is something I missed."

She didn't say anything at first. It looked as if his kiss had left her dazed. He wanted to take advantage of that look and tumble her back into bed with him and make love to her all over again. He was about to do just that when her next words stopped him.

"Your parents have agreed to watch the kids, which works out since they hadn't expected us back until Sunday anyway. I've called the airlines and booked the flight. We leave this evening."

Whoa, things were now moving so fast his head was spinning. He pulled himself up in bed. "Where exactly are we going?"

"Texas."

"Texas?"

"Yes."

He ran a hand down his beard. "Why?"

"To show you what I bought and that's all I'm saying about it. The rest is a surprise. And when you see it, you'll be okay with me buying it because it was a pardon, remember?" she said grinning. "Now I'm going into the bathroom to get ready for our day. We've got a lot to do." Before he could say anything, she'd slid off the bed and rushed into the bathroom.

As soon as the door closed behind Teri, Mac eased to sit on the side of the bed. Damn, he needed a cup of coffee. Black. A little gin in it wouldn't hurt, either.

What on earth had his wife bought in Texas? A purchase he'd pardoned. Had he spoken too soon?

He remembered the smile on her face and

how excited she was to share this surprise with him. He wanted to share her happiness, but that feeling of doom wouldn't go away.

Getting out of bed, he went to the coffeepot in the room and got it started. By the time he was sipping his first cup he'd figured it out. Teri had bought Tia a horse. That had to be it. He recalled her bringing up the subject of doing that last year, saying how well Tia was doing with her riding lessons.

Mac had squashed that idea when he'd made Teri see that not only did they not need a horse but they had no place to keep one. She'd come back to say the stables where Tia's lessons were held kept horses for other owners and for Tia to have her own personal horse to ride would be wonderful and a great ninth birthday present. He hadn't agreed and he had pretty much told her he hadn't wanted to discuss it any further. And they hadn't.

Had she gone behind his back and purchased the horse anyway? Knowing how he'd felt about it? Tia's tenth birthday was coming up in a few months and usually whatever gift they gave their daughter was a joint decision. Had Teri made that decision without him?

Mac pushed back the anger he felt, remembering he'd decided that when it came to Teri and any decisions she made without him, he wouldn't sweat the small stuff. But there was nothing small about owning a horse. Not the boarding of it or the cost of shipping it from Texas to Virginia.

"I'm back."

He turned around. An ache slipped through him and the lower part of his body hardened. She was standing there after having showered, a towel covering her middle. Barely. His wife was definitely acting the part of a seductress this morning. A very happy and elated seductress.

Had buying a horse for their oldest daughter and now knowing he wouldn't be blowing a gasket about it put her in such a happy mood? At that moment he knew if that was the case, then he would let her play out her surprise. Just seeing that huge smile on her face, something he hadn't seen in a long time, was worth it.

Placing his coffee cup down he slowly crossed the room to her and drew her into his arms. "Had I known you were taking another shower I would have taken it with you."

She laughed. "That shower gets us in trouble, Mac."

"But it's trouble we can handle."

She didn't look too convinced but eased closer to him anyway. "Did you forget we're supposed to go to the cabin today and look around?"

"No, I didn't forget," he said, pulling her closer to his naked body. "We have time and we will still make the flight to Texas."

"In that case…"

She reached up and cupped his face in her hand, leaned up and kissed him. He decided to let her do her thing before taking over. Mac liked the way she was using her tongue to entice him and when he was certain he couldn't handle it any longer, he swept her up into his arms and headed back toward the bed.

Teri squeezed Mac's hand as they stepped off the plane in Dallas, Texas. She glanced over at him. He'd slept on the plane during most of the fight and a part of her wanted to believe she'd worn him out that morning. If so, it would have been a first during the ten-plus years of their marriage.

After making love, they'd dressed and break-fasted downstairs in the hotel restaurant before leaving for the cabin. Seeing the wreckage had nearly broken her heart since she'd liked the cabin and enjoyed the days she'd spent there.

The tornado had flattened it, but Mac's duf-fel bag was located practically intact in a tree not far away. Most of Teri's stuff had been destroyed but she was happy when Mac had come across her driver's license and her house keys.

They had gone back to the hotel, packed and headed for the airport. Instead of heading for home they had caught a flight to Dallas. It was late and she'd booked reservations at a hotel. It would take an hour to drive to Terrell in the morning.

She still hadn't told Mac where they were going and he seemed okay not to ask ques-tions. He was going to accept the surprise she had in store for him. Now, as they drove to the hotel in the car they'd rented at the airport, she glanced over at him to ask, "You okay?"

"I'm fine. How long will we be in Dallas?"

She chuckled, wondering if he was trying to get her to spill her surprise. "Not long. You'll get your surprise tomorrow, after we get a good night's sleep."

She could tell from the look on his face that a good night's sleep wasn't something either of them would be getting.

"I miss the girls," he then added.

She missed them, too, but she knew what she had to show him and share with him would change their lives forever. And regardless of his so-called "pardon," she wanted to believe that after analyzing the benefits of owning a ranch he would see it was a win-win situation for them.

Once the pressure of having to tell him about the purchase had been lifted from her shoulders, she'd been able to closely examine the advantages of moving the kids from Virginia to Texas. And with Mac retiring in a couple of years, she could see him becoming a rancher. He could handle a horse just as well as she could and he would be his own boss. She couldn't help getting excited at the prospect, and a part of her felt she was insuring their future and their kids' futures.

They arrived at the hotel in Dallas, where she'd been able to get a suite, unlike the one they'd stayed at in Cheyenne. The moment the door closed behind them, he pulled her into his arms. The move surprised her. She had figured that, pardon or no pardon, he would be asking her questions by now, but he hadn't. It seemed as if it was her rodeo and he intended to let her ride it like she wanted.

And speaking of riding…

She liked riding horses but she liked riding her husband even more. Deciding to let him take control for a while, she accepted his kiss with the same hunger that he was showing. And when he broke off the kiss moments later to lift her into his arms and head for the bedroom, she wrapped her arms around his neck and buried her head into his chest. His masculine scent aroused her, made her want him in a way that had all kinds of sensations sweeping through her, rushing through her bloodstream.

And then every so often, he would lean down and devour her mouth with those barely-touch-your-lips kisses that literally curled her toes. When they reached the bedroom, he stood her on her feet and plowed her mouth with another kiss that made the earth feel like it was tilting on its axis.

"Mac…"

"What do you want, baby?"

She wrapped her arms around his neck. "I want to show you what I can do."

He smiled at her. "Then do it."

Having him give her the word emboldened her and she stripped off her clothes while he watched. She wanted him to watch. When she was totally naked, he began removing his own clothes.

"So tell me, Teri. Do you have a plan?"

Oh, boy, did she. Now if she could stop staring at his body long enough to regain her senses and put her plan into action. She followed the movement of his hands as they went to the zipper of his pants. She continued to watch as he removed his jeans to expose a pair of sexy black briefs. It was then that she saw he was every bit as aroused as she was. When he had completely stripped, she drew in a deep breath. Regaining her senses, she pushed him down on the bed on his back. Then she quickly straddled him.

"I'm about to put my plan in action, Mac."

"Baby, go for it."

She did.

Lifting her body, she eased down on his shaft, loving the way it felt inside of her. As soon as he was snugly there, to the hilt, she smiled down at him. She began moving, up and down, withdrawing in a way to set a rhythm that had him moaning, growling her name, as she rocked down on him with an intensity that drove her deeper and deeper with each downward plunge.

She'd become an expert horsewoman at sixteen and she was showing him just how well she could ride. It wasn't the first time she'd done so and it wouldn't be the last. She loved when she was in control like this, with him beneath her, taking her body while she took his. Just the way she liked and the way he wanted.

She felt so much love and desire. So much need.

From the first, when he'd introduced her to lovemaking for the very first time, she'd never wanted a man the way she did him. That thought rang through her mind every time her body lowered down on him and then lifted up. Her knees ground into his side and it seemed instead of reining him in, it spurred him to lift up the lower part of his body to meet hers.

Her fingers gripped his shoulders and his hands were wrapped around her waist. Suddenly, his hands moved up to the back of her neck to maneuver her head down to capture her lips. His tongue took control of hers and she could feel his heat, every ounce of strength within him and the full throttle of his masculinity.

Suddenly, a bolt of sensation struck her. She pulled her mouth from his to scream as an orgasm tore through her and she could feel the same rip through him. He quickly reclaimed her mouth and switched their positions where she was now beneath him, their limbs entwined, their bodies plastered together.

Moments later, when he broke off the kiss, she slowly opened her eyes and smiled at him. In a voice filled with sexual exhaustion, she said, "Plan accomplished, Mr. McRoy."

Mac woke the next morning to glance down at the beautiful woman in his arms. Their second round of lovemaking had completely worn out his wife—to the point where she'd immediately drifted off to sleep.

Easing out of the bed, he closed the door behind him and went into the sitting area to call his teammates. If he didn't, they would wonder why he hadn't returned home by now.

He told them about his surprise and what he'd guessed it was. Of course, Bane, Viper and Coop were excited at the prospect of Tia getting a horse. They would be, since they owned plenty of horses and the animals had been part of their lives for years. All three owned ranches and Bane had family members—a brother and several cousins—who raised and trained horses for a living. Mac admitted that after thinking about it, he'd decided Tia having a horse wouldn't be so bad. Especially since she did enjoy her riding lessons. Coop, who had a ranch in Laredo, even explained to Mac the best way to ship the horse to Virginia.

Mac recalled the horse that had been kept for him at his grandparents' ranch in Florida. Riding that horse had been the highlight of his summers each year, when he and his sister would leave the city to enjoy their time with their grandparents.

From the bright light coming in through the window, he figured it was about eight, and a glance at the clock on the nightstand confirmed it. He would let Teri sleep. Once she awakened, their day would get started. He figured, at least he hoped, she would take him to see the "surprise" so they could get back home to the girls.

"I love Dallas," Teri said, looking around after the waitress had taken their order.

They had decided to get out of the hotel to dine at a small café within walking distance.

What Mac liked about this particular café was that it was one of those mom-and-pop establishments and wasn't crowded. Only a few of the tables were taken.

He leaned back in his chair while sipping on his coffee as he gazed over at her. He'd drifted back to sleep after his phone call to his teammates and he and Teri had awakened just before noon. Hungry. He hadn't asked her anything other than how soon they could eat since they'd skipped breakfast.

"Do you?" he asked her.

"Yes. Have you forgotten I used to live not far from here?"

She was right. He had forgotten.

He'd never visited her in Terrell, where her grandparents' ranch had been located. But he did recall how hard the decision had been for her to sell it. "Yes, I had forgotten," he admitted. "I guess a lot of things bring back memories for you here."

"Yes," she said wistfully.

He reached across the table and took her hand into his. "I don't have a problem with that, just as long as they don't include an old boyfriend."

She chuckled. "They don't. If you recall, I was too busy trying to juggle both school and the rodeo to have a steady beau."

He did recall her telling him that one of her grandparents' stipulations about her involvement with the rodeo meant she had to also do well in school and college. Since education was important to him, he could see him making a similar stipulation with Tia if she ever decided she wanted to one day compete on the rodeo circuit like her mother had done. He'd long accepted the rodeo might be in his oldest daughter's blood and he was preparing for that day.

"I find that odd," she said suddenly.

He lifted a brow and looked at Teri. "You find what odd?"

"That man and his daughter. Their behavior."

He glanced across the room. The little girl who sat across the man appeared to be about eight. The two were eating breakfast and he didn't see anything the least bit strange about them. They were just two people eating breakfast.

"What's so odd about them?" he asked, looking back at his wife.

"She seems petrified of him."

Mac again glanced at the two. Again, he saw nothing amiss. The man seemed to be enjoying breakfast and the kid was not eating anything. In his opinion, the little girl appeared defiant, not afraid. "He probably laid down the law about something she didn't like. It happens, Teri."

"How would you know?" she asked, grinning.

"What do you mean how would I know?"

"That's what I'm asking. When have you ever laid down the law to your girls?"

He grinned back when he actually couldn't think of one single time. "I have good girls. I don't have to lay down the law. I lay it down to their mother, who I'm sure passes that law on to them when needed."

Teri rolled her eyes. "You come home after I've established the law and let them break it."

"No, I don't."

"Yes, you do."

Mac smiled. Okay, maybe he did. "So, I spoil them a little whenever I'm home. Is there anything wrong with that?"

"Yes, a lot."

He didn't want to argue with her about it right now and was glad when the waitress delivered their meal.

Teri clicked off her cell phone after talking with Mac's parents to check on the girls. According to them, everything was fine. Mac had gone to the men's room and she was slipping her phone back into her purse when her eyes fell on the table where the man and girl still sat.

She had tried not to stare, but more than once her gaze had been drawn to the two. Regardless of what Mac said, Teri was convinced something wasn't right. She was about to take another sip of her tea when the girl caught her eye while the man talked on the phone. There was a look in the little girl's gaze as they stared at each other. The man noticed the exchange and frowned at Teri, quickly clicking off the phone and saying something to the girl, who looked at him with what Teri felt was fear in her eyes.

Then, as she continued to watch them, the girl intentionally swept her plate and eating utensils to the floor. The man stood and grabbed the girl, nearly snatching her off her feet.

Teri was out of her seat in a flash and had crossed the room. "Turn her loose," she told the man.

He pulled the child behind him. "Do you dare to interrupt me chastising my child?"

"Yes, because if she was yours, you wouldn't handle her that way."

"Get out of my way, lady."

"No, I won't. Prove she's yours." Teri knew they were drawing stares and she didn't care.

"You either get out of my face so I can get my child out of here or I will—"

"You will what?"

Before he could respond the little girl said, "He's not my daddy!"

When the man turned as if he was going to give the child a slap, Teri pushed him and grabbed the child. Now it was the man hollering. "She took my child."

"What the hell is going on here?"

Teri immediately recognized Mac's booming voice. When the man tried to push Teri aside to reclaim the child, Mac intervened to protect her and shoved the man back instead, nearly knocking him to the floor.

"I asked, what the hell is going on?" Mac roared again.

"This woman took my child," the man snapped, straightening on his feet.

Mac looked at his wife, who had a furious expression on her face. There was no doubt in his mind she was ready to fight to shield the child if she had to. Teri Anne McRoy, the mother, was showing her protective colors.

Mac then looked at the little girl hiding behind Teri, who seemed to be holding on to his wife for dear life. He saw the fear in her small eyes. His gaze shifted back to Teri and before he could ask her anything, she got back in the man's face and said, "This child isn't yours. She gave me the signs."

"What signs?" Mac asked, trying to figure

out why his wife thought this girl was not the man's child.

Teri glanced at her husband. "The same ones I've told our daughters to make if they were ever taken against their will."

"She's crazy!" the man shouted. "That is my child."

"Prove it!" Teri snapped at the man.

Mac noticed the man had yet to ask anyone to call for the police. Leaning down to the child, who was still clutching Teri, he asked, "Is he your father?"

The little girl shook her head. "No. He took me from Mommy."

"She lies! She is my daughter!" the man shouted.

"Then prove it," Mac said, backing up Teri by making the same demand she had earlier. He noticed the other customers in the restaurant were evidently suspicious of the man's relationship with the little girl and were taking out their cell phones.

The man reached into his jacket as if he was going to pull out his wallet. Instead he pulled out a revolver and pointed it at them. "Give me the girl!"

Teri knew from the growl she heard from Mac that all hell was about to break loose. Mac could handle himself and would protect her. Teri's main concern was the child. When the man repeated his words, someone in the restaurant shouted, "The police are on their way."

That announcement angered the man. He tried reaching for the girl and Teri snatched back at the same time Mac moved forward, knocking the gun out of the man's hand before giving him a hard blow to the gut, sending him sprawling to the floor. When he made an attempt to get back up, Mac knocked him out cold.

"Teri, you could have gotten killed," Mac said. She heard the anger in his voice.

She smiled up at him before leaning up on tiptoe and kissing him on the cheek. "Not with my husband standing here protecting me. You're my hero."

She then looked down at the little girl and asked softly, "Are you okay?"

Instead of answering, the little girl threw herself into Teri's arms and cried. Moments later, the police burst into the restaurant.

Fourteen

Mac sat beside Teri at police headquarters while she gave a statement regarding what had happened in the restaurant.

The little girl had been reported missing that morning, snatched from her mother in broad daylight at a shopping mall. Instead of taking her immediately into hiding, the man had probably figured he had time to enjoy a meal first with her in plain sight. As Teri spoke to the police, explaining why she'd decided to come to the girl's aid, he could see obvious admiration and respect in the officers' eyes.

"His name is Leonard Caper and he has a

rap sheet a mile long. This was the first time he tried snatching a child. He's confessed to some guy paying him to do it, pick up any little girl. He's singing like a canary and we're following up all leads," a police detective was saying.

"Well. I'm glad he's off the street and I hope you get everybody who's involved."

"Yes, ma'am, we intend to."

Mac and Teri had met the little girl's parents. They hadn't wasted any time arriving at the police station to get their daughter. He doubted he'd ever met two more thankful individuals. The girl's mother had thrown her arms around Teri and cried profusely. Teri had cried, too. As the father of four girls he understood the father's need to get a piece of the guy, and more than one officer had to hold the man back from doing just that.

"If there's a trial, ma'am, you might be called back to testify," the detective added.

"I don't have a problem doing that if needed."

"Thanks, we appreciate it. And there is a ten-thousand-dollar reward for you, Mrs. McRoy.

It was set up by the Dallas Fire Department, where the little girl's father is employed."

Teri shook her head. "I don't want it. Give it to the parents to go toward the little girl's college education."

Even more admiration shone in the officers' eyes. "You will have to sign papers for that to be done."

"Sure, I can do that," Teri said.

Mac raised a brow when Teri turned to him with a worried look on her face.

"What's wrong?" he asked her.

"I hope not keeping that money is fine with you. We didn't discuss it."

"And there's no need. I agree with what you've decided to do. Besides, it was your money to do whatever you want with."

Teri shook her head. "No, it's our money. That's the way it is between us, Mac."

He knew that to be true. That was the way it was between them. Mac sighed deeply. They still had a lot of talking to do, things he needed to find out that he still didn't know. Namely, what she had bought that had her anxious.

One thing he'd discovered today was that his wife was capable of holding her own, even without him.

"Man, do us a favor," Bane said, as he and his teammates talked to Mac on the phone later that day. "You and Teri need to go home as soon as a flight can get you there. Instead of spending quality time together, the two of you are doing nothing but finding trouble to get into."

Mac couldn't help laughing at that, since it certainly seemed that way. They had finished giving their statements to the police but not before the news reporters had gotten there. "I'm just glad Teri picked up on the fact that little girl was in trouble. I hadn't suspected a thing."

"That just goes to show that she has certain skills you don't have, Mac. When will you realize you have a special woman on your hands?" Coop asked. "It's all over the news how she faced that man and took that girl from him."

That part angered Mac. "She could have

gotten hurt. That bastard had a gun." Mac didn't think he would ever forget the moment when that man had pulled his weapon out and pointed it at them. Namely, at Teri.

"And you got back in time to take care of business like you were supposed to do," Viper said.

"I'm going to make sure my daughter knows the signs when she grows up. People are messed up these days," Coop tacked on.

"Just the thought of that bastard assuming he could snatch somebody's kid like that," Flipper said. "It was a good thing you and Teri were there."

Mac nodded. "Well, it was almost too much action for me," he said. "I expect it as a SEAL but as a civilian? What's wrong with coming home to peace and quiet?"

"Nothing is wrong with it, unless you're married to Teri," Bane said, laughing.

Mac chuckled, knowing he wouldn't have it any other way. Moments later, after ending the call with his friends, he left the sitting area to go into the bedroom, where Teri was just clicking off her own phone.

She glanced up at him. "That was the folks. They saw us on television. The girls saw us, as well. They think their parents are heroes."

Mac smiled. "You mean they think their mom is a hero. You're the one who figured the kid was kidnapped. You want to tell me about these signs?"

She smiled over at him. "Keep your fingers on one hand crossed, and when you can, get someone's attention."

"And the kid did that?"

"Yes. She was sitting with her fingers crossed, and after you left, she knocked her dishes off the table, hoping to get someone's attention. But I was already on it."

"Apparently." He had walked out of the restroom to return to his table, only to find Teri confronting the kidnapper, with the child cowering behind her. He was certain that had he not knocked the man out then Teri would have done so herself. After ten years of marriage, he was surprised to be seeing his wife in a new light.

"Her parents told her what to do and she did

it. Like I told the police, she was a real trouper. If anyone was a hero, that little girl was."

"Well, more than ever I'm ready to go home," Mac said. "When are we going to see the horse?"

She lifted a brow. "What horse?"

"I figured that was the surprise. Am I right?"

She shook her head. "No, you aren't right."

He didn't say anything for a minute and then he asked, "Then what kind of surprise is there here in Dallas? What on earth could you have bought here?"

"Nothing in Dallas."

He lifted his own brow. "Then where, Teri?"

"In Terrell. I was able to buy back my ranch. So I did."

Mac stared at her, certain he'd heard her wrong. "Could you say that again?"

She nodded. "I got a chance to buy back my grandparents' ranch due to a 'first right of refusal' clause I had included in the contract when I sold it. That meant the current owners had to offer it to me first before they put it on the market."

"And you bought it?" he asked, incredulously.

"Yes."

He stared at her for a minute. "And how did you pay for it?"

She nervously licked her lips and he immediately knew that he wouldn't like her answer. Because he could think of only one way she could have paid for it. "Teri, how did you pay for it?" he repeated.

"I used some of our savings."

"Some of it?"

She shrugged lightly. "A big chunk of it."

He stared at her. "How much, Teri?"

"Not as much as you think."

"How much, Teri?"

"Remember your pardon, Mac."

"How much, Teri?"

She then gave him a figure that made him see red after his head began swimming. He knew how much they'd had in their savings and he now knew how much was left.

He thought about how long and hard he'd saved. How carefully he'd guarded each purchase. Yes, they had enough, but that money belonged to both of them and she hadn't consulted him at all. That money was for their future, for their girls. Generational wealth.

He didn't want them to worry the way he'd had to worry growing up.

He drew in a deep breath and then said, "The pardon is off."

She frowned. "You can't do that."

"I just did." He then walked out of the hotel room.

Teri froze the moment she heard the door slam shut behind Mac. He was mad. Furious was more like it. She had expected his anger days ago but when he'd said he would give her a pardon, she had believed him. He'd said it extended to her last purchase, no matter what she'd bought. Granted, a horse was definitely not as expensive as a ranch, but still…

And now he had left.

His usual mode of operation whenever he came home and discovered she'd purchased something he thought was outrageous would be to put distance between them to cool off.

Then he would return in an hour or so but ignore her for a day or two. Next would be the lectures, where he would do all the talking and like a disobedient child she was supposed to listen. Hadn't expressing how she felt over the past few days gotten her anywhere other than back to square one with him?

Okay, she would admit using so much of their savings was something she should have consulted him about since it had been funds set aside not only for emergencies but for the kids' education. Maybe wanting to buy back the ranch had been selfish of her. Had she put her wants ahead of her family's needs? It had been her decision not to keep the ranch years ago and it was a decision she should have accepted. She had for years, but then lately she'd begun regretting that decision, wishing she could offer their kids the same lifestyle that she'd had growing up. And she knew that moving to the ranch would be the right thing for all of them.

Granted, she should have consulted Mac, but he hadn't been available for her to do that. So she'd made the decision for them. He hadn't bothered to find out why. She would have gladly laid out the advantages if he'd given her a chance, but he hadn't. Now they had a ranch house that she wanted but he didn't. And she and the kids wouldn't live there without him. Was it wrong to want it all? The Ranch. Mac. She and the girls there with them. A happy family. A marriage that was not filled with arguments. Teri knew she would do whatever it took to keep them together. She would put him and their marriage first.

Getting up off the bed, she knew what she had to do. She grabbed her purse and reached inside for the business card of Jack Polluck, the man who'd handled the sale for her years ago and her recent purchase. Within minutes she was placing a call to him.

"Yes, Mr. Polluck, this is Teri Cantor McRoy. I want to put my ranch up for sale." She paused and then said, fighting back her tears, "Yes, I'm sure."

Mac tried to cool his anger by walking around a nearby park. He still couldn't wrap his head around the fact that his wife had bought not appliances, a new television or a horse. But a ranch. And she had used most of their savings to do so. What in the world had she been thinking?

And he hadn't bothered to ask her that?

He rubbed a hand down his face in frustration, realizing he was acting just like he usually did whenever he returned home from being gone for a long period of time to find the balance of their savings account less than what it had been when he'd left. He hadn't given her a chance to explain her actions.

He dropped down on a park bench. How could she explain buying a ranch in a state where he'd never lived? But then, she had lived here and evidently liked it enough to want to move back. However, after this morning, would he move to an area where kids could easily be snatched from their parents?

Mac was fully aware that he needed to be fair. He had to admit such a thing could have happened in any city in the United States. Even in Virginia. It was up to parents to prepare their kids and it seemed like Teri had prepared theirs. They knew how to give out signs. Hell, he hadn't even been aware of that. But Teri had.

What was it going to take for him to realize and accept that Teri had never bought anything foolishly? Whatever she did, whatever she bought, was something that would eventually benefit the family. He wasn't sure how a ranch in Texas would benefit them, but he was certain she would have laid it out for him if he had given her the chance.

And hadn't he pretty much acknowledged days ago that the recent problems in their marriage were more than her buying stuff? They included his habit of taking her and what she brought to their marriage for granted. He realized that, yet he was again doing that very thing. He stood up and began heading back toward the hotel. Determined that this time they would handle the situation differently.

When he got back to the hotel it was to find it empty with a note left in the middle of the bed.

Mac,

Sorry. Once again, I blew things. Even though I'd imagined we could all be happy there at the ranch, I thought more of my happiness than that of you and the kids and that wasn't fair. I've called the real estate agent to put the ranch house back up for sale and he feels certain he will be able to sell it for what I paid for it within a month or so. I'm heading back home to the kids.

Teri

He crumpled the paper up after hearing the defeat in her words. He glanced around. She was gone. For the second time in less than a week his wife had left him.

The key to the car was on the nightstand, which meant she'd taken a cab. He grabbed the key and headed for the door, knowing he was the one who was sorry.

Teri flipped through a magazine. She was on standby but she didn't mind waiting. She would rather sit here than be at the hotel with

Mac giving her the silent treatment. There was nothing left to be said. She hoped the note she'd left him explained it all.

Time passed. She was reading an interesting article and barely noticed the person sliding into the seat beside her until he said, "Aren't you tired of running away, Teri?"

She jerked her head up and stared into Mac's face. He wasn't smiling but then neither was she. "Why did you come here?"

He shrugged. "My wife is here and whenever I'm in the States, I like being with my wife."

"The same wife who likes spending your money?"

He chuckled. "Yes, that one. But then, my money is her money."

She rolled her eyes. "Yes, until she buys something. Why did you come here, Mac? I left a note."

"That note wasn't good enough."

"Well, it was for me." She then checked her watch. "Are you on standby, as well?"

"No. I came to get you. Our flight leaves out

tomorrow and not today. You were supposed to show me my surprise."

She jutted out her chin. "You said my pardon is over. So is the surprise."

He didn't say anything for a minute. "I want to see it."

"See what?"

"This ranch you bought."

"The same one that is now up for sale? Well, I have no desire to show it to you now. It doesn't matter."

He reached out and took her hand in his. "Maybe I need to explain something to you, Teri. Everything you do matters because *you* matter. I'm the one who owes you an apology. I know there're reasons for you to have bought the ranch and I need for you to tell me what they are."

"Why? The reasons won't change anything."

He shrugged. "Maybe not. But this time I'm willing to hear you out before passing judgment."

She lifted a brow. "Why? You've never done that before."

"I know. I'm honestly trying to do better. I

told you I was one of those works in progress. Why didn't you take me at my word? Why were you so quick to walk out on me?"

She looked away for a minute and then back at him. "Because I'm tired of fighting."

"We don't fight, Teri. We disagree. All couples do it from time to time. We shouldn't be any different."

"But we are," she implored.

"Then it's definitely something we should be working on correcting." He stood. "Come on. I want to see the place."

She looked up at him. "Do you really?"

"Yes. On the way there you can tell me why buying it was so important to you and how you believe it will benefit us and the girls. That's what's it's about, Teri. That's what it's always about with you. What's always in the forefront of your mind. I know that and truly believe you wouldn't do anything that wouldn't be for our best interest."

She fought back her tears. "I want to believe that, Mac. All I'm asking is for you to hear me out. And if you don't agree with my assessment after seeing it, then so be it—we will sell it."

He nodded. "Fair enough."

She then took his hand and stood. He gave her a wry smile and said, "I have a feeling I'm going to like it."

She lifted a brow. "Why do you think that?"

"I just do."

Fifteen

Mac did like it.

The moment he drove down the long driveway, he knew he was a goner. Probably before that, when she'd persuaded him to take the scenic route lined with large magnolia and oak trees and a number of bluebonnets. Then there were the lush meadows and valleys and the numerous lakes.

At one point he'd pulled to the side of the road, a part that had a beautiful view of the lake. He could see himself riding bicycles with the girls around here or having a picnic with Teri. He had visited Bane's, Viper's and Coop's spreads and he thought this place rivaled theirs in size and could be just as productive.

During the drive, Teri had made her pitch, and a pretty damn good one, too. She told him of the improvements the family that had last owned the ranch had made. They'd been improvements that had been needed but that she hadn't been able to afford, which was one of the reasons she had sold.

There was a spanking new barn and several small outbuildings that could be used as guest cottages whenever anyone visited. Another thing that impressed Mac was the size and style of the ranch house. Each of his daughters could have their own room with no problem. It was spacious and built in the ranch style he preferred.

He'd met the previous owners, who would remain in the house for the next couple of months. He'd done the figures in his head and would admit Teri had been able to buy back her home at a fair price, which showed just what a good negotiator she'd been in making the deal.

And this had been her home. The glow in her voice and the smile on her lips when she talked about it was a strong indicator of just what this home had meant to her. He hadn't known. After she'd sold the place, he had assumed she had walked away without looking back. Although that might have been true, losing her home had been a pain she'd refused to let surface. But it had been there.

She'd never admitted such to him, but it had been revealed in her voice when she'd told him of all the fond memories she had shared here with her grandparents.

Another plus that he hadn't yet shared with her was that his investment in Bane's family land management company, as well as their horse business, had showed a damn good profit last year and that had been passed on to the shareholders. That, along with his bonuses over the last two years, would be enough to replace the money from the girls' college fund, and they'd still have more than enough left over to start a business here. Already he could envision him going into the horse business with Bane's relatives, like Coop had done.

Even though they owned huge spreads, Viper and Coop had hired capable men to run things whenever they were gone. He could see himself doing the same thing.

"So, what do you think?" Teri asked, when they returned to the hotel hours later.

Closing his fingers around her wrists, he reached out and drew her to him. "Do you want me to be truthful?"

She ran a hand through her hair and sighed. "Not want, Mac. I *expect* you to be truthful."

He smiled, remembering when he'd made the same stipulation of her. "I will always be truthful with you."

Pausing a moment, he pulled her over to sit on the sofa. "You did good for your family, Teri. You might have thought of your wants with the purchase of the ranch, but you still considered the needs of your family, as well."

His eyes held hers. "I can see future growth here and generational wealth we can pass on to the girls. That's something I've always worked hard to do. It's why I took it so hard when you made purchases. Well, I can see it now. I can see this being a working ranch, one we can make profitable to pass on to the girls. I'm sure one of the four, maybe all four, would want to continue it like you wanted to do."

He reached out and took her hand in his. "Spending this week with you has opened my eyes to a lot of things, Teri."

She lifted her brow. "Such as?"

"What a lucky man I am. Hell, you saved my life in that mineshaft. I hadn't known a rope was under that trough or about any signs kids are taught in case they're ever snatched. In addition, you're pretty damn smart. I admit there was nothing you've ever bought while I was away that did not benefit us. I know you don't think I trust your judgment, but I do and I intend to do a better job proving it."

He decided to add, "That doesn't mean I won't ever question you about anything, because I might. When I do, please take it as my need to have more clarification versus questioning your judgment."

She nodded. "Thank you."

"No, I want to thank you. You're my wife, my partner, my soul mate and the mother of my kids. I love you, Teri. Don't ever forget that. Although I was upset about how you placed yourself in danger with that guy to get that little girl away from him, for you to have the guts and courage to even do such a thing showed just what a strong, capable woman you are. I am so proud to be your husband."

"Oh, Mac," she said, reaching out and cupping his beard, running her fingers through it.

He reached out and lifted her up to place her into his lap, wrapping his arms tight around her. "And another thing, I do want another baby, Teri. Like you, I didn't know how much I did until you told me about the son we lost. It doesn't matter whether we have a girl or a boy—I want to be a father again."

"Oh, Mac, I do want another baby, too, but what about all your concerns?"

"I believe in you. I know you will always do your best for all our kids."

"Thank you."

He'd entertained the thought of retiring in a few more years. Now that there was a ranch to run, they would run the ranch and raise their kids together.

"I don't think you know how happy I am

right now, Mac. I was so scared and worried. What I haven't told you is that I blamed myself for losing the baby."

"Why?"

"Because I lost the baby two days after I returned home from Terrell. I thought the flight had something to do with it, although the doctor said it didn't."

"And you should believe the doctor and not blame yourself for anything. I don't."

"You don't?"

"No, and you shouldn't, either."

"I love you so much," she said, before burying her face in his chest.

"And I love you." He stood with her in his arms. "And I intend to show you just how much."

He carried her into the bedroom knowing there would always be days when they didn't see eye to eye on everything, but at least they would agree on this one thing. They were a team.

And his wife would always be his to claim, just like he would be hers.

When they reached the bedroom, he placed

her on her feet. She reached up and wrapped her arms around his neck and pulled his mouth back down to hers. He had no problem giving her what she undoubtedly wanted. Namely, appeasing the hunger taking control of both of them.

He knew what she wanted and he was right there with her. Stripping his wife out of her clothes, he proceeded to do just that. His hands were busy, unbuttoning her shirt, then taking it off, unsnapping her jeans and letting her lean on him while he slid them down her hips. Her bra and panties followed and before removing his own clothes, he straightened and stared at the beautiful body before him. Her breasts were absolutely gorgeous and her waist small, even after four children.

He recalled that after Tia had been born, Teri had hated the stretch marks left from her pregnancy, but he had convinced her that any marks from giving birth to a child of theirs would be her badge of honor. A badge he appreciated her wearing and one he wanted her to do so proudly. After that, she never mentioned the stretch marks again.

"You know what I think?" he said, still staring at her. He was ready to do more than just look. He was ready to touch.

She smiled up at him. "No, what do you think?"

"That you're the most beautiful woman I know."

His words made Teri smile.

She was fully aware that other women found her husband sexy and could understand them doing so. She was cognizant of walking into rooms where women nearly drooled when they saw him. And she could honestly say she had never felt threatened. Mac made it a point to assure her how much he loved her and how beautiful he thought was. He said he didn't mind if his compliments ever went to her head.

He leaned down close to her ear and whispered, "And you know what else I think?"

"Um, you're on a roll, so you might as well confess all."

He leaned closer. "I think you would look even more beautiful pregnant again."

She fought back tears. For him to say that

meant he wanted to see her pregnant again. They had been using a condom for all their sexual encounters after being rescued. Was he hinting that he wanted to have unprotected sex with her again? That he was willing to not only risk her getting pregnant but also was hoping that she would be?

"I'm on board if you are, Mac. It will take two for that to happen."

He cupped her face in his hands. "Then let's get it on, Ms. McRoy."

He leaned down and kissed her breasts and when he did so, she closed her eyes and drew in a deep breath. When he sucked a hardened nipple between his lips she felt her breasts swelling in his mouth, making her moan.

When he pulled his mouth away, he said, "Not sure I'm ready to compete with my baby for these breasts, Teri."

Since she breastfed all her babies, she knew what he was referring to. "Poor baby."

He chuckled. "For some reason I don't think your sympathy is sincere. That means I'm going to have to torture you for a while."

Teri knew all about Thurston McRoy's type

of torture. She didn't want to admit it, but she loved it.

"Please don't." Inwardly she hoped that he would.

He bent down and licked his tongue across her stomach. When he did so, every cell inside her body flared to life. And when the tip of his tongue began swirling around her navel, she felt every nerve ending in her stomach flare to life. This was torment, and with every flick of his tongue she felt a pull, a tingling sensation between her legs.

As if he sensed her predicament, he glanced up at her and smiled. "You haven't felt anything yet, baby. Get ready. Here I come."

Getting down on his knees he stared down at the juncture of her thighs, and at that moment her legs began to quiver with the intensity of his gaze. He uttered a growl before leaning in and burying his mouth there.

Mac intended to show no mercy. Just pleasure. With that goal in mind, he used the tip of his tongue to stir a fervor within Teri, widening her thighs to capture the bud of her womanhood.

He took his time and showed no signs of letting up, intending to pleasure her. Even if it took all night. Already she was rocking her body against his mouth. He had no problem with her doing that since the more she rocked, the deeper his tongue intended to go.

Then he felt it, the first sign that she was about to come. Her thighs were quivering around him and when she suddenly threw her head back and screamed his name, he knew a maelstrom of pleasure was engulfing her. He could taste it.

When her trembling ceased, he stood and pulled her into his arms, capturing her at the same time his hand settled right between those legs.

"Now for something else going in here," he said, after breaking off the kiss. Using his fingers, he began stroking her there.

"You're torturing me again, Mac," she accused breathlessly.

"Guilty as charged," he whispered in her ear.

And then he edged her closer to the bed and

eased her down on her back and joined her there, sliding on top of her. Teri lifted her hips and Mac knew why and what she wanted.

Deciding he'd teased her enough, he eased inside of her, and instinctively, she opened her legs. Then he began thrusting in and out, back and forth. She moaned his name when he increased his strokes and he felt her body shudder again beneath him.

A growl escaped Mac's throat when he became caught up in the same pleasure he was giving his wife. Over and over, their bodies worked in unison as her hips rose off the bed at the same time his came down on hers.

"Mac!" She screamed his name when they both exploded in an earth-shattering climax that seemed never-ending.

He kissed her, slowly recovering from the effects of one hell of an orgasm and knew that before the night ended, there would be more, and all just as powerful.

Sixteen

Teri glanced across the table at Mac as they enjoyed breakfast at the hotel's restaurant. "What do you mean we aren't going home today?"

Mac smiled. "That's what I mean. Do you know that of all the days we've spent together this week, not a single one has been relaxing?"

She raised a brow, remembering all the hours spent in his arms making love. "So, you don't consider any of our time together relaxing?"

"I'm not talking about the lovemaking, Teri. I'm talking about just normal, uneventful time with you where we aren't trapped in mineshafts or you're not risking your life saving little girls or you're not showing me our future on the ranch. I want to go out and do something. Together. You like this area? Then show me why. The only time I've been to Dallas is when we came for Flipper's mom's birthday celebration. I didn't get to see much of it then."

Teri smiled, glad Mac was truly interested in the area she called home. "There's really a lot to do here. I can show you all my favorite places."

"Then let's spend the day together. When we go back up to our room, you can map out places for us to visit."

Teri appreciated Mac's thoughtfulness. Although he'd told her that he was looking forward to moving to Terrell, what he'd just said meant that he truly was. She would include getting together with Flipper and Swan in their plans since they were still in Dallas visiting Flipper's family.

After changing into more comfortable clothes and shoes, they hit the streets. They walked and checked out the Sixth Floor Museum at Dealey Plaza, a museum dedicated to the life and death of President John F. Kennedy. Since she was a history major, she was able to tell Mac a lot of things she figured he hadn't known.

They went to several other museums and the botanical gardens, as well. Holding hands, they walked through the gardens with rows and rows of both flowering and nonflowering plants.

"Do you think the girls will have a problem leaving their friends?" he asked her when they left the gardens to head out to the Reunion Tower.

She was excited about taking him on the high-speed elevator ride that went to the top in sixty-eight seconds. It had always been a fun place for her while growing up.

"I think they will at first, but I also think they'll love it here and make new friends. I can't wait for them to see it," she said.

"Neither can I."

After visiting a number of other sights, they drove into Terrell, and she took him around town. News had traveled fast about her buying back her family farm and everywhere they went people told her how glad they were that she'd decided to move back home. They visited her old high school and she even took him to the rodeo school where she'd learned to rope her first calf.

She knew Mac had an ulterior motive for wanting to meet some of the people in Terrell. He would be gone for long periods of time during covert operations and needed the peace of mind that she would have a similar network of friends in Terrell like she had in Virginia. He soon saw that this was home for her and everyone in the area around the ranch knew her and looked forward to her return. He mentioned that he was glad Flipper's parents lived close by, too, in Dallas.

Teri was happy, too. She was excited to meet Flipper and Swan for lunch. The couple were thrilled to hear that Teri and Mac had bought back the ranch that had been in Teri's family for years. Flipper and Swan had their own good news to share. They were expecting their first child. Teri was happy for them. She would never forget how Flipper had risked his life by swimming into that flooded mineshaft to save them.

Later, on the drive back to the hotel that evening from Terrell, she tried calling Mac's parents to check on the kids. When she didn't get an answer, she turned to Mac. "That's odd."

He looked over at her when he brought the car to a traffic light. "What is?"

"I can't reach the folks."

"What's odd about that? This isn't a school night so they probably took the kids out for pizza or something. You know how the girls wrap them around their fingers."

Teri chuckled. "If anybody knows about their ability to wrap someone around their fingers it would be you. The girls have you wrapped so tight it isn't funny."

"Whatever. And about it being not funny, you don't hear me laughing, do you?"

Teri smiled. "Although I totally enjoyed our time together today, I really miss the kids."

"I do, too, and I enjoyed our time together, as well. We need to do it more often. How does the idea of date night sound?"

"It sounds great and the Wilkersons' daughter turns seventeen this year, and old enough to babysit for us. She's smart and levelheaded."

Once they got back to the hotel, they stopped at the ice-cream shop and enjoyed a bowl of ice cream together. When they reached their hotel room, Mac opened the door and then stepped aside for Teri to walk in ahead of him.

"Mommy! Daddy!"

A surprised Teri shrieked upon seeing the girls and raced across the room to give them hugs. She gave her in-laws hugs, as well. She then turned to Mac. "You arranged this?"

He grinned as he walked across the room to give her a hug, since she was obviously in a huggy mood. "Yes. I knew that although you were enjoying my company, you were missing the girls as much as I was. I called Mom and Dad after you went to sleep last night and made arrangements to get them here."

"That's why you kept me away all day?" she asked, grinning back at him.

"No, I kept you away because I wanted to spend time with you," he said, leaning in and kissing her across the lips.

"Do we really have a ranch, Mommy?"

"Will we have horses?"

"And plant our own food to eat?"

"And make new friends?"

All the questions came at them from the girls seemingly at once. Together Mac and Teri answered each and every one of them to the best of their ability, although the reply to a number of them was "We'll just have to wait and see." It was important to them that their girls looked forward to making the move as much as they did.

"So when can we see this ranch?" Mac's father asked, and Teri could hear the excitement in his voice.

"Tomorrow," Mac said, wrapping his arm around Teri's waist. "I talked to the owners and they are looking forward to showing you around."

"And it's the house where you lived as a little girl, Mommy?" Tia asked her.

Teri smiled down at her daughter. "Yes." She wished she could tell Tia about her and Mac's plan to get her a horse, but she knew it would be a surprise. Tia had a birthday coming up and that would be soon enough to share the news.

School would be out for the summer in three weeks and they intended to put their current home up for sale and begin packing. They hoped to be settled in at the ranch before school started in the fall.

That night when they went to bed, Mac held her in his arms. He had arranged for the girls and his folks to have a hotel room next door with a connecting door. It was hard to deny Tasha when she wanted to stay and sleep with them, and Teri was surprised Mac couldn't be charmed by their youngest daughter. Usually he would give in to her, but this time he didn't. He told Tasha that she needed to stay with her grandparents because Mommy and Daddy needed time by themselves together. Teri could tell Tasha didn't agree, but she left with her grandparents anyway.

"Thanks for bringing them here," she said to Mac when they were alone in bed. She wasn't dumb. At some point during the night Tasha would get out of bed and knock on the connecting door. And when she did, Mac would get out of bed, open the door and let their daughter into their bed to sleep with them.

"You were missing them and so was I. Besides, the folks wanted to see the ranch. It was the perfect time."

"And your parents are perfect with them."

"I have to agree with that," he said. "I have a feeling we'll be seeing a lot of them once we move to the ranch."

"I hope we do. We'll have plenty of space at the house, or they might prefer one of the cabins for privacy. One thing is for certain, we'll have plenty of room."

"We will definitely have that." He then pulled her deeper into his arms.

When he leaned down and kissed her, every part of her yearned for him, aching in a way that had the area between her legs throbbing unmercifully. "I hope you know sooner or later we're going to get a little knock on that door. Tasha never takes 'no' as an answer, especially when it comes from her daddy. You know what that means, right?" she asked Mac.

He grinned. "Yes, I know what that means. We don't have any time to waste."

Mac pulled her to him and kissed her, and she nearly drowned in the masculine essence of him. Something he always said rang through her mind.

She was his to claim. Now. Forever. Always.

Epilogue

Five months later

Bane Westmoreland opened the door and smiled at the couple standing on his doorstep. With the arrival of Mac and Teri, all his team members were accounted for.

"About time you guys got here," Bane said, leaning over to give a very pregnant Teri a kiss.

"Stop complaining," Mac said. "Teri doesn't move as fast these days as she used to."

Teri glanced over at her husband and frowned. "Don't you dare blame me for us being late, Mac, when you refused to move from in front of the television until that football game was over. I tried to get you to leave the hotel an hour ago."

Bane shook his head since it was obvious Teri was in a tiff about it. "I see it's business as usual with you two."

"Not exactly," Mac said, grinning and wrapping an arm around his wife's protruding stomach. "We found out yesterday before leaving home that we're having twins. Both boys."

"Congratulations!" Bane said, happy for his friends. "Now, get inside so everyone can congratulate you two, as well. Six kids. Wow!"

Mac grinned proudly. "Yeah, that's what I say. Wow! The good thing is my folks love the ranch and are crazy about the cabin we're giving them. They will move in soon. Mom's going to be a big help to Teri and our six kids while I'm away."

Bane nodded, smiling. "Sounds like you two have things worked out. After having only three kids I understand how important extra help is."

Mac, Teri and the girls had moved to their

ranch in Texas a couple of months ago. Of course the SEAL team members had been there to help. Their ranch would be a horse ranch, and thanks to Bane's family, who owned a horse breeding and training company, already several horses had been added. Like Coop's ranch, Mac's would also serve as a horse depot that housed the animals before they were shipped off to be trained. There was even some discussion about later making Mac's ranch an official horse training site. The partnership was proving to be a financial incentive for Mac and Teri.

Since Mac was still on active duty, one of the Westmorelands' foremen, who wanted to move closer to his son, daughter-in-law and grandkids in Dallas, had accepted the job as Mac's foreman. The McRoys' ranch had been named Timberlake, a joint effort by their daughters.

Mac had surprised his wife last month. On her birthday, he had given Teri a special gift. A horse. Namely, Amsterdam. Upon discovering how much the horse had meant to Teri, Mac had bought it from the owners of the

Torchlight Dude Ranch. Mac had also bought horses for each of his daughters.

Tonight they were all gathered to help Bane and Crystal celebrate their move to their new home on "Bane's Ponderosa," his stretch of land in Westmoreland country. Once Mac and Teri were inside, no introductions had to be made. Bane's teammates knew all of his family members, those living in Denver, Atlanta, Texas and Montana. They also knew the Westmorelands from Alaska—who went by the last name of Outlaw.

Also present tonight was the newly elected local sheriff, Peterson Higgins, better known to everyone as Pete. Pete had been best friend to Bane's brother Riley and Bane's cousin Derringer since grade school and was like a member of the Westmoreland family.

Bane and Crystal circulated around the room and Bane couldn't help noticing that the two senators in the family, Reggie Westmoreland and Jess Outlaw, had their heads together discussing a piece of legislation they intended to pass with the help of their colleagues.

A couple of other Outlaws—Garth and Cash—were talking with Bane's brothers Dillon and Canyon and his cousin Riley, hashing out how their two companies, the Outlaw Shipping Company and the Westmoreland Land Management Company, could benefit each other.

In another corner of the room, Teri was getting tips about what to expect with the birth of her multiples from Bane's wife, Crystal, and Nick's wife, Natalie, both mothers of triplets, and Bane's brother Jason's wife, Bella, who had twins.

Bane was happy for Mac and Teri. Mac would be retiring as a SEAL in a couple of years to become a full-time rancher and Bane knew his friend was looking forward to it. With Teri and six kids, Mac would certainly have a lot of help.

The doorbell sounded and Bane wondered who the latecomer could be. With the arrival of Mac and Teri, he'd figured everyone on his and Crystal's guest list had already shown up. Giving Crystal a sign that he would get it, he moved to the door and opened it to find an older couple, who appeared to be in their late sixties or early seventies, standing there with a baby in their arms.

Bane was certain he did not know the couple. "Yes, may I help you?"

The man spoke. "We hate to impose but we were told Peterson Higgins was here tonight. We are the Glosters, his deceased brother's in-laws."

Bane nodded. "Yes, Pete is here. Please come in."

The man shook his head. "We prefer not to, but we would appreciate it if you could tell Peterson we're here. We would like to speak with him. We will wait out here."

Bane nodded again. "Okay, just a minute." He circled around the room before finally finding Pete in a group in the family room, discussing motorcycles with Bane's cousins Thorn, Zane, Derringer and one of the Alaska Westmorelands—Maverick Outlaw.

"Excuse me, guys, but I need to borrow Pete for a minute," Bane said to those in the group. Once he got Pete aside, he told him about the older couple waiting outside. Pete placed his cup of punch aside and quickly moved toward the front door.

Bane wasn't sure how long Pete had been gone, but when he returned he was carrying a baby in one hand and a diaper bag in the other. Everyone's attention was drawn to Pete when the baby released a huge wail.

It seemed all the mothers in the room hurried toward Pete. "Whose baby?" Bane's cousin Gemma was the first to ask, taking the baby from a flustered-looking Pete.

"This is my nine-month-old niece, Ciara," he said, noticing how quickly the baby girl quieted once Gemma held her. "As most of you know, my brother, Matthew, and his wife, Sherry, were killed in that car crash six months ago. This is their daughter. Sherry's parents were given custody of Ciara when Matt and Sherry died. But they just gave me full custody of her, citing health issues that are preventing them from taking proper care of her. That means I'm now Ciara's legal guardian."

Pete looked around the room at the group he

considered family and asked the one question none of them could answer.

"I'm a bachelor, for heaven's sake! What on earth am I going to do with a baby?"

* * * * *

Note from the Author

I want to take this opportunity to thank Kim James for sharing her experiences and challenges as a military wife with me in order to give greater depth to my heroine, Teri McRoy.

And to all military wives everywhere, you are deeply appreciated for serving your country right along with your enlisted spouses. We honor you. Thank you so much!

LET'S TALK

Romance

For exclusive extracts, competitions and special offers, find us online:

f facebook.com/millsandboon

⊙ @millsandboonuk

🐦 @millsandboon

Or get in touch on 0844 844 1351*

For all the latest titles coming soon, visit millsandboon.co.uk/nextmonth